MIDW

Leaving a busy hospital to work as an
independent midwife was a drastic move,
but Melanie Aarts knew it was the right
step to make. If only she did not have to
fight the hostility of her own professional
colleagues—as well as the disturbing
Dr Daniel Davenport . . .

X

Kate Ashton was born in Scotland. She was brought up in England but returned to Edinburgh to train as a Registered General Nurse, specialising in ophthalmics.

After spending some years on the staff of one of the professional journals for nurses, she decided to write independently from home. She says that writing Doctor-Nurse Romances gives her the pleasure and privilege of sharing both the real world of nursing and her dream-world.

MIDWIFE MELANIE

BY
KATE ASHTON

MILLS & BOON LIMITED
15–16 BROOK'S MEWS
LONDON W1A 1DR

First published in Great Britain 1985 by Mills & Boon Limited

© Kate Ashton 1985

Australian copyright 1985 Philippine copyright 1985

ISBN 0 263 75322 0

Set in 10 on 10½ pt Linotron Times
03–0286–60,200

Photoset by Rowland Phototypesetting Limited Bury St Edmunds, Suffolk Made and printed in Great Britain by Richard Clay (The Chaucer Press) Limited Bungay, Suffolk

For Ali Lems, my midwife

CHAPTER ONE

'But I can't spend the rest of my life in hospital!' wailed Melanie.

'You make it sound like prison,' her flatmate smiled. She looked at Melanie's stricken face.

'I daren't tell you before that I'd handed in my notice,' Melanie continued, 'because I knew you'd try to put me off, and I might have listened to you.'

Rachel stood up from the kitchen chair, stretched and filled the kettle. When she had put it on to boil she faced Melanie again. The older girl of the two, Melanie was dark-eyed and fresh-faced. She wore her long hair up most of the time, swept away from her fine dark brows and strong features in a classic, almost black chignon at the nape of her neck. There was an intensity in her face which often made her flatmate rue her own soft prettiness.

'I can't believe it.' Rachel shook her fair curls and gazed at Melanie. 'I thought you were really happy at Lessing Lane.'

'I am—I mean, I was,' Melanie admitted carefully, 'but it isn't the hospital as such, Rachel, it's the patient care . . .'

Rachel erupted into affectionate laughter, got up again and went through the time-honoured ritual of tea-making.

'Is that all? Patient care! Well, what has *that* got to do with hospitals?' she giggled ironically.

'It's serious, Rachel,' insisted Melanie.

'I know it's serious. Midwifery is midwifery,' said her flatmate firmly, 'and there are good and bad practitioners wherever you work.'

'That's true,' Melanie sipped her tea, 'but is the

practice of midwifery as good? Even the best practitioners are restricted by fossilised tradition.'

Rachel looked hurt.

'I don't feel fossilised or restricted,' she said. 'I think
Lessing Lane's a super place. From the Prof down the
medical staff are enlightened and easy to work with, and
they all respect the staff midwives, even if they get a bit
snooty with the pupils sometimes.'

'A bit snooty sometimes,' muttered Melanie almost
inaudibly, 'that's generous.' She struggled to redirect
her train of thought from its inevitable destination. 'It's
true,' she managed, 'on the whole they're a decent
crowd of doctors and they don't—generally—treat us as
though we've no right to be at the bedside. But that
doesn't mean that they fully appreciate our potential.'

'He really got your goat, didn't he?'

Melanie flashed Rachel a warning glance, but Rachel
grinned cheekily back at her.

'*He* can't be your reason for going, Mella? He'd be *too*
flattered to hear of his effect on you.'

Nobody was more adept than Rachel at rubbing salt
into a new wound, and nobody more honestly innocent
of her ability. Melanie flinched. She knew that Rachel
remembered the staff meeting only too well. She could
see the amusement dancing in her flatmate's lovely blue
eyes as she relived it.

She visualised once again the calm appraisal to which
the new consultant obstetrician had subjected her while
she stood in the middle of the room about to present
'her' case to the monthly meeting. She had prepared
herself well for the presentation and did not normally
suffer from nerves before her colleagues, but today was
different. For some reason the room seemed empty but
for that implacable presence in the middle of the front
row.

Daniel Davenport had been on the staff at Lessing
Lane for precisely one week. He was staring at her as
though he had not met her, but in fact they had already
had one encounter in the ante-natal clinic on the morn-

ing of his arrival. Melanie heard her own voice introducing her case: 'Mrs Macgregor, a twenty-five-year-old
prima gravida, was admitted with a six-hour history
of acute indigestion at twenty-six weeks . . .', but
all she was aware of was the muscle that twitched in Dr
Davenport's cheek while she noted with almost clinical
dispassion his thick fair hair, firm mouth and the fine
lines at the corners of his grey-blue eyes.

Her own voice continued as if disembodied while he
returned her look, his head gently inclined to one side as
though each move and every word from her received his
scrutiny. When her ordeal was over at last, she found she
was trembling.

'Thank you, Staff Aarts. Most interesting. And the
infant's thriving, isn't she?' The Professor directed his
question at the little cluster of midwives from the Special
Care Baby Unit, and it was Rachel who provided him
with the facts and figures on Baby Macgregor which
satisfied him. 'Thank you, Staff.' He smiled pleasantly,
evidently happy to go on with the proceedings.

After ten years as medical chief at Lessing Lane,
Malcolm Young had a reputation as a brilliant and
radical obstetrician with fresh new views on the psychology of infertility, pregnancy and maternity. He had
published several books which had won him popular
acclaim and he was regularly invited to broadcast his
opinions on national radio phone-ins and television
feature programmes.

Prof. Young encouraged autonomy in his midwives
and listened to and responded to their professional
views. It appeared that his new addition to the senior
medical staff was going to be less respectful. Dr Davenport was on his feet, commanding audience attention
with a lift of his eyebrows. The muted chatter which had
broken out in anticipation of the next case presentation
died away. The new consultant stood easily, relaxed,
and his leonine masculine grace shocked Melanie into a
dread of what he was to say. She knew he would address
himself to her and she did not know how she would cope.

'The type of abdominal pain . . .' he began slowly and deliberately, fixing her, 'Miss—er—Aarts . . . You do not specify the type of abdominal pain complained of by this patient. You used the word 'indigestion', but the pain associated with premature labour is severe, continuous and situated in the lower abdomen. The word "indigestion" suggests mild, cramp-like upper abdominal discomfort . . .'

'The patient described it as "indigestion", sir,' Melanie responded. 'It was the only presenting complaint.'

'"Indigestion",' repeated the consultant infuriatingly. Melanie frowned and felt herself colouring.

'What she actually said, sir, was that ever since breakfast her belly had been "awf'y sair" . . .'

A burst of laughter greeted Melanie's faithful imitation of her patient's Glaswegian accent. She met Dr Davenport's steady gaze without flickering. To her surprise, he smiled engagingly at her.

'We must try to avoid paraphrasing patients' complaints, don't you agree, Miss Aarts? Especially when we have such charmingly complete recall of the actual words used . . .'

There was another burst of giggles amidst which the consultant calmly resumed his seat. Melanie glared at him and then sat down herself. Confused and furious at the memory, she now flushed once more to find Rachel's eyes upon her face just as they had been that fateful afternoon.

'He's quite a lad, our Daniel Davenport,' mused Rachel. She had been watching her flatmate's expressive face for some time and now had the satisfaction of seeing her jump out of her reverie.

Rachel cleared the table, then followed Melanie and leaned in her bedroom doorway while she changed. Melanie pulled her jersey dress up over her head, then paused to pull out the hairpins which had caught in it as she did so. For a moment she was arrested in mid-undress, and irritated by it. It's that bloody man, she thought furiously and irrationally, the mere mention of his name is enough to ruin my day! She emerged from her dress, red-faced, her dark hair tumbling down over her shoulders.

'Oh, you're there!'

Rachel's smile was quizzical.

'I just wondered,' she began teasingly, 'where you'd been in all that finery.'

Melanie pulled on a pair of jeans and a striped cotton top, then an Arran sweater.

'To see a real midwife,' she smiled sweetly.

'I see!'

'No, seriously, I'll tell you about it, if you really want to know, Rachel?'

'Of course I do! Don't treat me like an arch-enemy. Keep that for those that dare! I am your sworn friend. But I worry sometimes.'

The two girls settled themselves a couple of seconds later each into the depths of the two capacious armchairs which graced their living room. Outside the large bay windows of the Edwardian first floor flat the wind rocked the bare branches of an old walnut tree.

It had been a mild winter and a sunny snowless Christmas had just gone by. January looked as if it would pass in a flurry of fallen leaves and blustery rain. London, especially west London, so rich in trees, was at its best in autumn and in spring, and this year it seemed as though winter had decided not to intervene.

Melanie met Rachel's expectant stare and took the plunge.

'I spent the whole afternoon with Bridget Reid, an independent midwife who practises from her home near Hammersmith. I got her name from a girl I met at a study day. She was a bit radical and I was rather worried about taking Bridget's name from her at all, but as soon as I met her I knew it was the right thing to have done.'

Melanie paused, but Rachel was listening raptly.

'It was a big step to telephone her. She invited me to

come and see her today. I went to the practice and
looked at how she works. Then we talked for hours
non-stop about everything from fathers to follow-up
visits and marriage to motherhood. We liked each other
right from the start—at least,' Melanie corrected herself
quickly, 'I liked her. She's a really wonderful person,
Rachel, so warm and strong and really committed to her
work.'

'Is she married herself?'

'Yes, but she doesn't have any children yet.'

'Does she want a partner so that she can have her own
baby?'

'No, I don't think so. I think she wants to build up the
practice first and she needs a partner for that. She's
already overbooked, and more and more women seem
to want to have their babies at home. They love the
continuity of care. Some want her to see them through
their pregnancy and then to deliver them in hospital too,
so it's really their choice.'

'And do I assume that if she asks you to join her you'll
go?' asked Rachel seriously.

'Yes.'

'Do you think you'll be happy working out on a limb
like that? With nobody to back you up or advise you
both?'

'Oh, Rachel, what's the use of a hundred people
advising you and backing you up if you feel the system
itself is wrong?'

'None,' admitted Rachel doubtfully.

'You know what the worst thing is?' confided Melanie
quietly. 'I'm losing confidence in myself. The more we
seem to mystify the patients and intervene the less I
seem to be able to practise midwifery the way I want to,
and the less of a good midwife I feel I am.'

'That's bad,' said Rachel.

'I know.'

'And so tomorrow's your last day at Lessing Lane. I
can't believe it!' Rachel shook her head again, but this
time there was candid affection in her cornflower-blue

eyes. 'Well, let's hope there are no breech deliveries or brushes with you-know-who!'

Melanie ran down the stairs and picked up the envelope that lay on the front doormat. It had been delivered by hand. She tore it open on the way into the kitchen where she put two pieces of toast into the toaster before reading its contents.

> 'Dear Melanie,
> It was super to meet you and I've decided not to stand on ceremony. I'd very much like you to join me as a partner in the practice. Please could you ring to confirm the starting date we discussed. Looking forward to hearing from you,
>
> > Bridget.'

It was the nicest, most amazingly informal offer of a post that she had ever received in her years in nursing and midwifery. It seemed to produce an answering cry inside her that convinced her that this move, though drastic, was right.

And yet she loved the Health Service and she hated to leave it. All through her training, first as a State Registered Nurse and then as a midwife, she had sworn lasting allegiance to a health care delivery service which had been founded on her deepest-held beliefs.

But she had waited five long years before training as a midwife; five years through which she had questioned the strength of her vocation, examined her own motives and finally understood and fixed her own maternal feelings. She believed that a midwife needed to be mature in herself. Having come so far, she could allow her own professional growth to be stopped by the very system which had first inspired her.

She spread butter and then honey on the toast she had just made and put more bread in the toaster. Rachel bounced into the kitchen as she took her first mouthful.

'Well?'

Melanie handed her friend the note and watched her face while she scanned the contents. 'Are you pleased?'

'Of course I am, Mella. Well done! I hope you'll be really happy. But we'll miss you at Lessing Lane.'

'It'll be quieter without me.'

'Well, there is that!' smiled Rachel.

A few minutes later they caught the bus which carried them majestically slowly up towards the centre of the city. Long before the streets lost their trees, though, and the strange salty smell of the river was lost, they got off and walked the rest of the short journey to the hospital.

The South-West City Hospital sprawled almost the length of a whole street, the white research block of the huge teaching hospital dominating the district. Drawn in, like an ancient grandmother into the heart of her family, lay the grey stone façade of the original hospital which had been built more than a century before. Although it was almost lost now amongst the pre-fab units and new ward blocks, it was this old centre that lent the hospital its lasting air of dignity.

Lessing Lane itself stretched leanly down one edge of the original hospital building until it met the maternity annexe to which it had given its name. These modest, homely buildings were all which occupied the lane and they were grimy with age. On the opposite side of the lane stretched a much neglected but pleasant park, play place for local city children, home for many a scrawny cat and, in summer, green retreat for the gaze of busy maternity staff and patients alike.

Melanie surveyed the bare trees, languishing grass and empty benches of the park, and then the warmly-lit windows of the old 'lying-in' hospital. How she loved it today!

'I'll miss this place,' she whispered.

'Don't worry, I'll keep you in touch,' promised Rachel.

They greeted the hall porter, who knew each and every midwife by her first name and never abused the privilege.

'Morning, Staff Aarts and Staff Lewis,' he nodded, 'nice day for the time of year.'

The old cage lift which took them up to Labour rattled and hesitated between two floors.

'Not today!' prayed Melanie aloud.

'What's so special about today?' enquired Anne Brown, who had joined them in the lift on the first floor. She was a forthright redhead who worked on the post-natal ward.

'It's Melanie's last, that's what,' replied Rachel.

Suddenly Melanie realised the full truth of the fact that nobody knew. She had gone through the agonies of the damned to reach her decision to leave Lessing Lane and she had resigned in deepest secrecy. Now she faced the job of justifying herself to her friends and colleagues, and she did not relish the prospect. To say nothing of saying goodbye to them all.

'You? Going? You're joking!' said Anne unself-consciously, 'but you're the most dedicated midwife on the staff!'

'Thank you,' smiled Melanie, 'if that's a compliment?'

The lift clanked to a standstill as Anne smiled her answer. The three midwives stepped out with their usual sense of relief that the journey had been successfully completed. Anne, having asked Melanie where her admin. post was, set off purposefully in the direction of Sister's office while Melanie and Rachel turned into the small staff changing room.

'Well, you can bet that that isn't the message that she came up to give Gracie. Not that that'll make any difference.'

'Oh, lord,' moaned Melanie, zipping up her fresh pink dress and adjusting her frilled cap, 'and I haven't even spoken to her yet. I didn't think I could face telling her until I'd got a job to go to. She'd have thought I was even more crackers than she already does!'

Rachel winked at her friend.

'Saved by the post!' She handed Melanie her letter from Bridget. 'You left it next to the toaster,' she said.

Sister Grace Ewing gave the new shift a swift and full report on the stage and condition of each of the four women currently in labour under her wing, and allocated each to the care of one of the midwives for the day or until she delivered.

Then she turned to Melanie.

'What's all this I hear?' she asked. It was obvious that she didn't know whether or not to believe Anne.

Melanie waited until the other girls had dispersed before explaining properly what she had done and why. Sister listened attentively. When Melanie had finished speaking, she smiled.

'I don't know what we'll do without you, Melanie,' she said, 'and I didn't know why the Allocation Officer had given me an extra staff midwife either.'

'I'm so sorry not to have told you, Gracie . . .'

The older woman's features softened. 'Don't worry about it—I understand. This place is no respecter of secrets. I've not heard about independent practice, so I'll expect you to keep in touch and keep me up to date,' she smiled.

Melanie nodded, and thought she was dismissed, but Sister Ewing put a gentle restraining hand on her arm.

'You'll have an outlet for some of your creative talent as a midwife, by the sound of it. And that can't be anything but a good thing,' she said softly.

Melanie was almost overcome. Sister and she had always been good friends, almost without verbal confirmation of their mutual respect for each other as midwives.

'Thank you, Grace,' she said.

'Don't you dare not come back and see us!'

Melanie got down to work with difficulty, her normal concentration and application disrupted by the emotion of knowing that she was doing everything for the last time. But there were only two straightforward deliveries between the beginning of the morning shift and her lunchtime, so it did not matter too much that she was slower and more thoughtful than usual. Melanie waited for Rachel to come up from the Special Care Baby Unit and they walked together to the staff canteen, then queued for sausage, egg and chips. They took their trays to a table already half full.

'So,' began Tessa Fulbright, Sister-in-Charge of the ante-natal clinic, the minute they had sat down, 'are you really deserting us, Melanie?'

'Yes,' Melanie responded with the new confidence that her conversation with Sister Ewing had given her, 'I'm going into independent practice.'

'What's that?' queried Tessa. 'Private, I suppose. Lots of lovely loot for sitting about all day delivering the odd film star?'

'No,' said Melanie, 'it's not like that at all. It's just working outside the National Health Service, giving midwifery care to women, that's all. I doubt if there's much sitting about,' she added, annoyed, 'nor many film stars, either.'

She was almost more nettled by her own ignorance than by Tessa's silly remarks.

'Apparently there's little or no medical supervision, either, according to Anne.' A tall blonde midwife with large green eyes contributed her addition to the conversation with evident satisfaction at the new aspect it uncovered. She was new to the staff at Lessing Lane and worked in Post-natal under Anne Brown.

'There's no necessity for a midwife to work under medical supervision, Tessa. Didn't they teach you that at your training hospital? A midwife can work alone, according to the law. You should know that.' Rachel spoke with uncharacteristic ferocity, and everybody turned to look at her.

'I know that. But . . .' Anne joined the group, placing her tray firmly down on the table opposite Melanie's place and looking at her while she spoke, '. . . we all know who carries the can if anything goes wrong.'

There was a moment in which nobody spoke, then Melanie said, 'A midwife is accountable for herself, to her own professional body—and anyway, none of us, least of all me, is in any position to discuss independent practice. I'll come back and tell you all I've learned in a few weeks' time.'

She hoped her modest words would defuse the atmosphere around the table, which was frankly hostile. But inside she was shaking. If her own professional colleagues were so suspicious of anything new, how could she find the courage to care for a woman through her normal pregnancy alone? What if they were right and she could not cope with any problems that cropped up and which were easily managed on a ward? She made up her mind that she would be very cautious with her new responsibilities, and if . . .

'Melanie's partner is very experienced,' Rachel was saying as if to close the speculation and silence the chatter that had broken out around the table, 'and it's nothing new for midwives to work unsupervised by doctors. They always did, you know, before the brave new age of 1985 . . .'

In the quietness that greeted this remark Melanie realised as if for the first time what a good friend she had in Rachel Lewis.

'I didn't really have a chance to thank you for what you said at lunchtime,' Melanie told her as they left the hospital some five hours later.

'You don't have to,' Rachel replied.

'I want to. You were super. I was feeling really fragile for some reason.'

'Goodness knows how I'll feel the day I leave Lessing Lane. It's like the proverbial womb. It was a shame your farewell party was such a muted affair, but it was the best Gracie and I could do—with so little notice.' Rachel dug her elbow accusingly into Melanie's ribcage just as they were about to take their places in the revolving doors that led outside and into the Lane.

'It was lovely,' said Melanie when they were out in the crisp January afternoon. 'Thanks for the roses, Rachel. I know they were your idea.'

'Wrong!' said Rachel, 'mine was the medallion. Grace got the roses during her lunch-break.'

Melanie cradled the flowers with care. She was already wearing the silver necklace with which she had been presented by her ex-colleagues. She felt an obscure sense of disappointment over the flowers. It was ridiculous and ungrateful, she knew, but she appreciated flowers always with the bitter-sweet sense of regret that nobody had ever really given her any—no man, that was.

'Anyway,' Rachel continued goodnaturedly, 'everyone seemed to come around to the idea that you were leaving us in a reasonably good cause, except old Danny, that is . . .'

'Dr Davenport?' Melanie said quickly. 'He wasn't even in the department.'

'Oh yes, he was. I meant to tell you. He appeared just after you'd gone down to say goodbye to the folk in Ante- and Post-natal. While Gracie and I were clearing up after your tea. At first he was vastly amused at catching us playing housemaid—you know what he's like: superior smile, slight lift of the eyebrows, etc., etc.—but when he heard the reason for it he changed his tune considerably. He wasn't too well pleased with your surprise departure.'

'How do you know that?' asked Melanie, swallowing the swelling which had risen in her throat.

'Just the subtle hints he dropped,' grinned Rachel, 'like asking Grace if she planned to let all her best midwives go the same way. And what the hell was "independent practice" anyway?' Rachel giggled. 'Verbatim report.'

Melanie tried to suppress the nervous content of her answering smile.

'He must have been up all night delivering someone, poor soul,' she suggested, 'although goodness knows he doesn't seem to think he needs an excuse for belligerence.'

'He thought he had a good one this afternoon, that's

for sure,' Rachel replied, and gave her flatmate a long sideways look.

'Here's the bus.' Melanie boarded it with relief and stowed herself and her bouquet carefully into a window seat. She wanted to forget Dr Daniel Davenport. She did not know why he and she reacted together, or rather upon one another, in such an unsympathetic way, and she certainly felt in no mood to discuss the matter. If she had, Rachel would have been the last person to whom she would have turned.

Rachel thought her flatmate needed a man. She had been a little quieter about this of late, since the end of her own last love affair, but Melanie knew that this was simply a stay of execution and not a reprieve. As soon as Rachel met someone else she would begin again, not least to cover her disquiet at leaving her friend alone in the flat evening after evening. It was always the same: Rachel would pounce on the name of a male newcomer or newly released partner in their professional or social circle and urge Melanie to put herself in his path.

Melanie described this trait to herself as Rachel's only fault, and she treated it with indulgence. But sometimes it hurt. For some reason she felt that it was about to hurt if Rachel talked any more about the new consultant obstetrician at Lessing Lane. She comforted herself with the thought that she would be seeing little or nothing of the man from now on. Rachel's fantasy could burn itself out naturally. She looked into her red roses and bit her lower lip.

'And this is where I keep all the stuff I take to delivery. It's all set up, packed and ready to be grabbed at short notice: sterile instruments, intravenous infusion equipment, laryngoscopes for resuscitating babies and all the usual obstetric drugs. I take Pethidine with me always, and Entonox, but my clients hardly ever need or want painkillers. The electric foetal monitoring machine goes with me, of course, and my bleep so that I can be contacted at any time by any client or doctor.'

Bridget paused and glanced at her new partner. Melanie, after a weekend off during which she had been too excited to rest much, was taking everything in as she had been doing for the past two hours.

'Coffee?' offered Bridget. She watched the magic word take effect. 'It's a lot to take in, isn't it?'

Melanie dropped into an easy chair in the large room adjacent to the consulting room. 'It's just that it's all so different,' she replied.

She did not tell Bridget that she could hardly imagine what it was going to be like working with her. She looked around the pretty room, full of potted plants and dark brown cord upholstered chairs, pictures on the walls. The atmosphere was so quiet and calm—so utterly unlike the warm bustle of the clinics at Lessing Lane. She would have to change her own working pace and attitude.

Bridget put a plate of biscuits and two cups of coffee down on the table in front of Melanie. She brushed her cropped brown hair back, watching Melanie steadily. 'It'll take a bit of getting used to,' she said, 'I took ages to adjust. But the real thing is having confidence. Confidence in the women who come to us and in ourselves as guardians of the natural birth process.'

'What do we actually do at a delivery?' Melanie ventured.

'I never know!' laughed Bridget. 'I just have to wait and see what happens and adjust myself. Each birth is unique and different from any other. But I do all the usual monitoring and apart from that, keep a low profile, guided by what the mother needs from me.'

'I hope I'm up to it,' Melanie ventured.

'Of course you are!'

There was not much more time for wondering. The morning's clients began to arrive almost the minute the two midwives' coffee cups were empty. Melanie sat nearby while Bridget saw each one, testing her early morning sample of urine for sugar, acetone, protein and blood, then taking time to talk to her about how she was feeling both physically and emotionally before weighing her and checking her blood pressure.

Each woman climbed up on to the examination couch for Bridget to palpate her abdomen, checking the size and position of the baby before listening to its heartbeat with the electronic as well as the simple aural foetal stethoscope.

Everything was unhurried and quiet. There was plenty of time for the woman to tell of her worries or fears, plenty of opportunity for information to be given to her. Melanie kept having to pinch herself to remind herself that the woman in a white overall was a midwife and not a doctor. Several times she had to remind herself that she was at work. It was so strange to be introduced to each client by her name and for them to see her as simply another woman in ordinary clothes. She realised that her hospital badge and frilled cap had served so often to distance her from her patient rather than bring them closer together.

Later, she told Bridget this.

'I used to feel so lost, never knowing how someone I'd delivered was doing afterwards,' she went on. 'I used to worry about how their stitches healed, how they were getting on with their husband and whether they were managing to breastfeed all right.'

'So did I,' said Bridget, 'but that's the marvellous thing about practising like this—you know all these things. And the sense of fulfilment is fantastic.'

Three o'clock in the afternoon arrived and Bridget sent Melanie home. When she tried to point out that she had only been on duty since eight, Bridget laughed.

'Stop thinking like a hospital nurse,' she advised, 'and be grateful. You'll work more hours with me than you've ever worked in your life, covering the twenty-four hours each day. Tomorrow I start you off in earnest. Only one day's induction here. Normally, I don't go in for them at all.'

Melanie knew that what she said was true. They had already discussed the long erratic working hours in-

volved in the practice, and the fluctuating income, and
Melanie had decided that the advantages outweighed
the disadvantages.

She decided to walk home to Bedford Gardens. The
air was fresh, the afternoon clear and she thought she
could smell spring in the air. Her mind was full of her
new job. She had hardly been able to believe her luck
when Bridget had asked her to start today. After the
rather lukewarm send-off she had had from her colleagues at Lessing Lane, Bridget's enthusiastic welcome
had felt like a homecoming.

And she had finally done it: gone independent. After
all the years of weighing up the pros and cons, after all
the frustrating incidents and minor battles which had
characterised her midder training.

It was honestly not that Melanie disapproved of
modern obstetrics; she did approve. But she felt it
should be practised with care and respect for a natural
process, so that the value of any medical procedure was
more than the risk to mother or baby. And she had seen
mothers frightened; surely that was avoidable?

Turning from a side street into Chiswick High Road,
Melanie found herself looking into the windows of a
florist. Green containers of shining red and yellow tulips
stood on the pavement beside her—the first of the
season's hothouse flowers from Holland. She had a vivid
mental picture of the ribbons of colour running across
the flat land of her childhood memory.

Her father's sister Ineke, who lived near Amsterdam,
had always been her favourite aunt. As she grew older,
though, Melanie's affection for her had taken on a new
dimension. Ineke practised as a 'free' midwife in
Haarlem and she it was who had first inspired Melanie
with her joy in her work. Ever since her midwifery finals,
Melanie had promised herself a visit to see her aunt and
talk with her, but there had never been time, or money,
or both.

Now she renewed the promise to herself. Tonight she
would write to Ineke and tell her everything; her move

from Lessing Lane and all about Bridget. Why hadn't she thought about it before? She would get all the support and confidence she needed. Almost without thinking, she went into the shop.

'Two bunches of tulips, please,' she told the girl, 'one red and one yellow.'

I'll take them into the practice tomorrow, she thought, as a lucky omen for my first real day. The remainder of her long walk down the High Street was spent wondering how she was going to explain the difference in atmosphere between Bridget's practice and the clinic at Lessing Lane to a still sceptical Rachel. The fact that she had just actually walked into a florist and bought herself two bunches of flowers with not a hint of her old nostalgia did not occur to her.

The next morning, Melanie woke up with a strange sense of lightness, remembered her new job and jumped out of bed. She dressed, luxuriating in the choice of her dress as only one who has worn uniform all her working life can. She put on a beige corduroy skirt and toning shirt, slipped on a sleeveless jersey and notched a dark brown leather belt around her slim waist.

She put her hair up as usual and looked at the overall effect in the mirror. A woman! She had had to admit to herself her sadness the last time she had put on her pink Lessing Lane uniform. Now she looked at her new professional self with pride and interest, as if her new job began here, in front of her bedroom mirror.

Arriving at the practice, her arms full of tulips, she was just remembering Bridget's words about work beginning in earnest today when she heard her partner calling to her from the consulting room.

'Melanie? Don't take your coat off!'

'Is there a delivery?'

'Not *a* delivery, *your* delivery,' Bridget grinned, shoving a bag into Melanie's hand and relieving her of her flowers. Melanie was suddenly in possession of a set of keys for a brand new Mini Metro.

'You can drive,' Bridget informed her.

'Where to?'

'Bedford Park,' replied Bridget, 'and she's well into second stage already, so we'd better get a move on. I waited for you.'

Melanie drove as fast as she could through the receding rush hour traffic. The client lived three streets away from her own flat, and she recognised her face from the local shopping area.

They arrived just in time to deliver a little dark-haired baby girl. The sun shone uncertainly in through the windows of the newly-painted nursery room while Melanie bathed and dressed the tiny creature in a new nightdress. The first size, it was still much too big for her.

'Why did she leave it so long before calling you?' Melanie asked as she opened the passenger door for Bridget a little later.

'She felt confident that all was going well and, as you saw, it was. But most women call me long before they reach that stage,' said Bridget, smiling at Melanie's alarmed expression. 'Don't worry!'

Back at the practice, the two midwives wrote up the notes for the patient whom they had just delivered, going through her ante-natal care for Melanie's benefit. She saw how the couple had prepared themselves for the birth of their child and began to understood how calm they had been during the birth. Education seemed to be everything when it came to confidence during the birth.

A steady stream of clients passed through Melanie's hands during the afternoon, and she conducted the routine ante-natal examinations with growing confidence herself. A plump redhaired woman put her head nervously around the consulting-room door just before four.

'Come in, Edna,' encouraged Bridget. 'Edna Dupont, this is Melanie Aarts, my new partner.'

'Nice to meet you, dear.'

It was impossible to guess at what stage Mrs Dupont's

pregnancy was, so naturally round was she, but her anxiety was much more easy to discern.

'It's my ultra-sound, Bridget dear. I'm so nervous,' she admitted.

Bridget sat her client down gently but firmly.

'Melanie,' she said, 'what do they do at an ultra-sound examination?'

Melanie carefully described the procedure, stressing that it was completely painless and that the mother could actually see her baby while it was in progress. When she had finished talking it was obvious that Edna Dupont was much more relaxed.

'Well, is that what I told you last week, or isn't it?' asked Bridget kindly.

'Almost word for word,' admitted Mrs Dupont.

'Would you like Melanie to go to the hospital with you?'

The woman smiled at Melanie.

'If she's got time, that would be lovely,' she said shyly.

'I'd love to come,' Melanie asserted.

'I'll see you next week then, Edna. And you tomorrow, Melanie. Take care of each other!'

Melanie picked up the folder of notes Bridget had pushed towards her across the desk and stood up. She did not have time to read the notes now, but something told her that she would soon hear the full story from her client.

Once more she slipped behind the wheel of her new car and drove off in the direction of Chiswick High Road. But this time she took the turning off next to the South-West City Hospital and parked neatly in an empty corner of the gravel car park in front of Lessing Lane maternity annexe.

CHAPTER TWO

'. . . AND SO, you see, I thought I'd have the second one at home. But I was so frightened to tell the doctor, I'd thought he'd be so cross, so I left it a long time before going to see him,' concluded Edna Dupont.

'But when you did he was quite happy about it and recommended that you go and see Bridget?' Melanie checked the car doors and ushered her client towards the familiar building. 'And now the only problem is that nobody knows how far gone you are?'

'That's right, dear. But the family doctor, Dr Robertson, he was so nice—and so young. He's new,' Edna explained.

Melanie had to still a stab of nostalgia as they waited for the lift. She was glad that it was late afternoon and the hospital was quiet. It seemed to take its own nap about this time each day, just as the early shift trickled off duty and the patients settled down to sleep off the effect of their afternoon visitors.

At the first floor Melanie stepped out and held the heavy iron doors open for her patient.

'Ah! What have we here? A wanderer returned to the fold?' A warm smile lit the features of senior registrar Joe Peters. 'Welcome!' he added.

'So you've heard. I couldn't find you the day I left, but they said at Reception you'd gone off for some reason. Excuse me, Edna,' Melanie interrupted herself, 'but I only left here last week.'

'Oh, don't mind me, dear.' Edna lowered herself gingerly into a rather small plastic chair in the waiting area of the ante-natal clinic.

'Delighted you've found an outlet for your talents at last,' said Joe. 'Gracie told me all about it.'

Melanie looked into Joe's lean face and thought how

27

much she liked him. He was very tall and very thin, bespectacled and scholarly, but his cheeky smile belied his serious appearance. He had been a good friend to her at Lessing Lane. He shared many of her views on the medical staff's treatment of patients—they had been professional accomplices, sharing jokes against the less liberal medical and midwifery staff and generally enjoying one another's professional company.

'How's it going?' he asked.

'Fine. But it's nice to be back inside Lessing Lane, even if it's just for an hour or so.'

'And what can we do for you?' He looked kindly down at Edna.

'It's a special sound test, Doctor.'

'Confirmation of dates, Joe,' explained Melanie, passing him Edna's notes.

'Ah, you're our last ultra-sound for the day, are you? Well, you're going to enjoy that. I bet you haven't seen your baby yet, have you, Mrs Dupont?'

Edna allowed herself a nervous smile. 'Not yet, Doctor.'

'Well, now you shall. We can go up right away. Just come this way.'

Joe took Edna by the arm and led her to a small room at the far end of the clinic. Melanie followed them in—and looked straight up into the face of the person she had least wanted to meet today.

Daniel Davenport acknowledged her presence without surprise or enthusiasm. Then he took Edna's notes from his junior colleague and scanned their contents. What on earth he was doing in the ultra-sound room Melanie could not imagine. It was late and the technician could well have gone home by now, which could explain Joe's presence. But the consultant? Her mind hovered unconvincingly over the possibilities; he must be doing some research or other.

'Now, if you'll just get your things off and settle yourself up on this couch, Mrs Dupont, we'll take a look at this baby of yours.'

Melanie listened to his voice in her head while she helped her client to undress and get up on to the examination couch. The presence of the man in the room with her muddled her thinking and distracted her. Even when she was not actually looking at him she was acutely aware of everything he did.

'You see that little screen, Edna?' she whispered, taking her warm damp hand in her own, 'that's where you'll see the baby's shape appear.'

Dr Davenport wheeled round at the sound of her voice and she caught his icy glance. She concentrated all her attention on soothing Edna, whose bare abdomen lay exposed, surrounded by equipment which sprouted wire.

'The doctor's just going to put some oil over your tummy then run that thing that looks like a microphone over it. You won't feel anything except the pressure of it.'

Joe smeared olive oil over Mrs Dupont's abdomen, wiped off the excess, and moved the screen a couple of inches to the right.

'There. Can you see that now?'

'Yes, thank you, Doctor.'

'Now, keep watching.'

'Twenty-four weeks,' murmured Daniel Davenport as the ultra-sound probe tracked back and forth.

'Look,' said Melanie, 'you can see his head—that shadow there—and his back curled round on the left side. Can you see, Edna?'

'Yes! Oh, how lovely!' Edna whispered. She wiped her eyes, then watched the flickering image again. 'Oh, he's moving!'

'He's probably wondering what on earth's going on,' said Joe, with a warm look at his patient's moist eyes.

The consultant was still watching the screen, assessing the size of the foetal head with practised skill. He said something to Joe in a low voice, then wiped Edna's abdomen clean of oil and told her he was finished.

Melanie pulled up the sheet, then helped Edna down to the floor and into the dressing room.

'So you're glad enough of an obstetrician when you can't tell the duration of a pregnancy, are you, Miss Aarts?'

Melanie met the consultant's withering look with all the conviction she could muster.

'I've never denied the invaluable contribution of the obstetrician,' she responded. She wished with all her heart that Joe had not just left the room with the records that had just been taken. A light remark from him would balance what had been a silly speech from her. Why, oh, why did she always end up feeling pompous and right-eous in front of this pompous and righteous man?

'Well, that wasn't anything, was it, Mrs Dupont?'

Melanie's client had emerged, dressed and smiling, and put an end to their encounter.

'Thank you, Doctor,' said Edna, 'I hope everything's all right, Doctor?'

'You're six months pregnant, Mrs Dupont, almost to the day. And you've a fine healthy baby . . .'

'Oh, don't tell me, Doctor! I don't want to know!'

Dr Davenport's face softened. He looked with amuse-ment at Edna's embarrassed expression and Melanie noted the transformation when he smiled. There was something young and tender in his face which vanished the moment he composed his features again. The grey-blue eyes retained their warmth only for a moment, then reverted to their cold habitual distance.

Edna Dupont was still blushing.

'I meant, I don't mind if it's a girl or a boy, Doctor, just so long as it's all right . . .'

'I know, Mrs Dupont,' Dr Davenport responded gently, 'I was merely telling you that the baby appears to be quite healthy, from this test.' He leaned near her confidently, kindly, and Melanie could not help smiling. 'I don't know its sex either,' he admitted in low tones to the patient.

Mrs Dupont looked surprised. 'Don't you, Doctor?

Well, thank you very much, Doctor. Six months!'

Melanie followed Edna out of the room.

'Thank you, Dr Davenport,' she said politely as she did so.

'Oh, thank *you*, Miss Aarts. Any time.'

It was a dismissal. Melanie turned and met the cold smile for a second, then turned her back on him.

'Come on, Edna,' she said, 'I wonder where Dr Peters got to?' She swallowed hard. 'I think he went off with your notes.'

Joe met them in the clinic, looking even taller and thinner now that he had discarded his white coat and appeared in a pinstripe suit. He handed Melanie Edna's notes.

'Thanks, Joe,' she said, 'I hope I see you again soon.' Relief at her release from Daniel Davenport's presence put extra warmth into her voice.

'Yes, and that reminds me . . .' Joe watched Edna disappear into the Ladies nearby, 'Don't you forget how you stood me up at the Christmas Party and promised me the May Ball instead. Come to think of it, I'll give you a ring next week. We'll have a jar together and discuss changed circumstances.' He winked enigmatically.

Melanie watched her client re-emerge, adjusting a bright green headscarf over her mop of red hair.

'All right, Joe,' she said quickly, 'that would be really nice.'

It really would be nice, she realised, almost with surprise, as she watched Joe indicating the deserted clinic to Edna.

'First to arrive and last to leave, that's me.' He mopped his brow, and Edna looked suitably impressed.

Melanie shook her head with a smile. Joe sprinted for the lift with a wave, and Melanie and Edna followed him at a more dignified pace. Melanie was thinking that he was not quite the last member of the medical staff to leave Ante-natal that afternoon. She was aware of Daniel Davenport sitting in the ultra-sound room, going through recordings and writing up notes. There was something about him that had disturbed her today, something that reached her below his rudeness and apparent desire to insult her.

'That's a nice young doctor,' remarked Edna. 'He quite put me at my ease. And so dedicated.'

'Yes,' said Melanie absently, 'Dr Peters is sweet, isn't he?'

She looked with irritation at the long white Porsche which had nosed its way in like a cat and now lay alongside her Mini in the corner of the car park. There was hardly any room now for her to squeeze in and open the door on her side, and none on the other for her portly client.

'Some people just don't think, do they?' she commented. 'Just a minute, Edna. I'll back out, then I can let you in.'

She didn't recognise the white car, although only Lessing Lane staff and ambulances were allowed to park in the forecourt. It wasn't until she was reversing and turning to face the lane that she noticed the West Country number plates on the Porsche.

There was only one member of staff whose car this could be: Daniel Davenport. Yet he was upstairs in the ultra-sound room and the car had arrived while they had been busy. Quite against her will, Melanie's heart fell. Of course! His wife must have the use of the car during the day.

She screeched to a halt just behind the gates. Edna Dupont! What was the matter with her? She had almost forgotten her. She opened the passenger seat door and waited while Edna slowly plodded down the gravel path towards the car.

'Where did you say you lived?' she asked when her client was comfortable.

Her mind was half on the driving and half on something quite different. The set of a strong chin, high cheeks and a small movement in a masculine jaw haunted her homeward journey. She kept seeing his eyes. His face was of the type that stays youthful for a long time and suddenly ages into granite maturity. His physique carried the same quality of full-grown strength.

But there was something else about Daniel Davenport which Melanie had felt for the first time today; that he had suffered in some way, that something had stopped his carefree smile and changed him for ever. She felt sure of it, and she could not stop wondering what it could have been. It was as if her independence from Lessing Lane had given her a secret licence to think about him which she had not allowed herself before.

Nobody knew anything about him there, though rumours were rife. Ever since the imposing figure of Daniel Davenport had first arrived on the scene the midwives of Lessing Lane had been busy inventing his private life. It was not an easy task. There was so little information to go on. In the six months since he had appeared from a small hospital in the West Country —was it Elchester?—he had failed to show his face at a single hospital social function. Lessing Lane was famous for its staff parties, outshining every other unit at the SWCH, yet even Christmas had failed to draw the new consultant out of hiding.

It was said that he'd specialised in obstetrics and gynaecology late, after beginning a promising career in general surgery. And it was true that he looked slightly older than the average consultant in his first post. Melanie guessed him to be in his early forties. But this was all that the grapevine could yield on the new man, try as it might.

His marital status remained a subject of controversy, the general consensus being that he was married or perhaps just divorced. He certainly showed no interest whatsoever in the female staff of Lessing Lane, a fact which both irked and intrigued them. Melanie had listened quietly to the speculation, smiled politely at the mischievous jokes and kept her own mouth firmly shut.

She was unused to experiencing the awareness that she felt of this man's presence. She had worked coolly for ten years with doctors, some of whom had been very handsome and many flirtatious. They had not moved her an inch. But Daniel Davenport had been different. He had seemed almost to seek confrontations with her and had seemed irritated by almost every move she made. Well, now she really had moved. And surely that would be that.

When Rachel got home to the flat after eleven that night she was surprised to find Melanie still up and sitting in darkness in the living room. The steady amber light from a street lamp outside softly illuminated her face. Rachel sensed that she did not want to be disturbed. She whispered goodnight, but she could have sworn that Melanie had been crying.

'It's a final post-natal visit, so I shouldn't be more than an hour or so,' said Bridget.

'Don't worry, I'll be fine. I can handle things here, I think,' said Melanie.

She had been working in the practice for a full month now and her confidence was increasing with her experience. She no longer dreaded Bridget's brief instructions or her regular departures from the practice. She had been on call herself and understood how deliveries were often at short notice. It was amazing, but she had almost forgotten what it had been like to work in any other way.

Bridget picked up her black bag and slipped her coat on. 'If you're quite happy, I might do a bit of shopping on my way back. We're quite quiet here this morning.'

'Do,' said Melanie.

'Oh, I know what I was going to say: the next client who appears—a new one, that is—is yours. You can take her through from start to finish. Your first complete case.'

'Oh, here we go!' groaned Melanie, 'I bet she'll have everything and need a Caesar at the end of it all!'

'Optimist!' retorted Bridget. 'See you later.'

Melanie started to set up the consulting room for ante-natal visits. She put clean paper sheeting over the examination couch and plugged in and tested the electronic foetal heart monitor. Test tubes for blood specimens were prepared for women to take to their general practitioners as this was the only test that the midwives did not do themselves. Urine sample testing sticks were set out on the trolley along with disposal containers and all that was needed for specimen collection. Melanie checked the disposable gloves, specula and swabs, the presence of the hand foetal stethoscope and the sphygmomanometer for measuring maternal blood pressures.

While she set everything up, she thought about her first patient; the first woman whom she had ever known that she would see through from her booking visit at the ante-natal clinic to the final post-natal appointment, six weeks after the birth of her baby. It was a thrilling thought—what she had waited for all through her midwifery career.

But it wasn't only the midwives who suffered from the present system, she reflected. Melanie had heard countless women complaining that they never saw the same doctor or midwife twice running on their visits to Lessing Lane. This was often nothing more than an inconvenience, but it could be more of a problem when a woman was worried and in need of consistent information and reassurance.

It could be lonely, this way of working. She had discovered that she missed the bustling companionship of work on the units of a busy maternity hospital, but to be able to see a patient through her pregnancy uninterrupted—surely it would be worth everything.

She jumped at the sound of the doorbell. A couple of seconds later she opened the door to a tall, slim, green-eyed woman with a mass of beautiful flaxen hair piled high on her head. Beneath the open dark fur coat, she was elegantly dressed, and her smile was confident and friendly.

'Come in,' Melanie invited. There was something about the woman which she recognised, yet could not place. It was as if she had seen her somewhere recently, but the memory had a dreamlike quality.

The woman followed her into the coffee room where new patients were seen. Melanie knew she had not attended the practice before, but she was not at all sure that she was even a prospective client. She took the woman's hand and shook hands formally with the stranger.

'I'm Julia Young,' she said simply. 'How do you do?'

Professor Young's wife! Melanie's mental picture of the woman focused itself sharply. She had seen her sitting with her husband at the more formal social functions at Lessing Lane. She had been struck then, as now, with Mrs Young's cultured beauty and her astonishing height, which she carried with the confidence of one who knows her own strengths. She had presented a calm and striking appearance beside her animated, wiry-haired husband, whose stature was smaller than her own.

'Melanie Aarts,' responded Melanie softly, 'Bridget Reid's partner. Please do sit down, Mrs Young. I'll bring you a cup of coffee.'

She took the luxurious coat and hung it up on her way to make the coffee. Returning with it, she braced herself for what she dreaded, yet suspected had to come next.

'Don't I recognise you from somewhere?' asked the cultured voice. Mrs Young's frank gaze swept Melanie's face. Here goes, she thought.

'Yes, you might,' she began. 'I was a staff midwife at Lessing Lane up until a month ago. I worked in your husband's labour ward and post-natal unit. He is a really marvellous man to work with,' she heard herself adding with sincerity.

'Yes, isn't he?' Mrs Young agreed cheerfully and unselfconsciously. 'I used to work for him myself. Before I married him I was the Senior Sister on the labour ward. A long time ago!' she laughed. 'I was Gracie Ewing's predecessor.'

'Were you really?' exclaimed Melanie. Mrs Young looked as if she had spent her youth gracing society coming-out balls rather than labour rooms.

'Anyway, I'm jolly glad to be under the care of one of Malcolm's ex-midwives. I don't mind admitting it inspires extra trust in me . . . and perhaps it'll even have the same effect on him . . .' she screwed her face up comically so that Melanie was left in no doubt as to the situation.

'So you're going to have a baby?' she ventured, stupidly. She felt like pinching herself in case she had relapsed into dreaming again.

'Of course I'm going to have a baby!' retorted the Professor's wife, 'and I'm going to have it at home. I'm a perfectly terrible case for you to take on—an elderly prima gravida, thirty-eight years old, whose husband does not approve of home deliveries, and a midwife into the bargain! And we all know what sort of patients nurses and midwives make: the worst sort.' She smiled winningly. 'So you can expect trouble. But I'll try not to be too much of a know-all. And I'll work on Malcolm,' she promised.

Melanie smiled, in spite of herself. She was still shocked at her own sheer ill-luck, and yet there was something so open, charming and lovable about Julia Young that somehow she was already looking forward to having her as her client.

'Well, Mrs Young, while we're exchanging confidences, there's something I have to tell you too. You should know that you'll be the very first patient whose care I follow through from start to finish. So it's a first for me too.'

'Excellent!' declared Julia Young. 'I think we shall get on famously together. You can begin by calling me by my first name—please. You really must try to forget whose wife I am.'

'That might be easier said than done,' admitted Melanie, 'but I'll do my best. Now, please tell me why you want to have this baby at home and how many weeks pregnant you are, first of all. I'll make some preliminary notes, and we'll leave the routine examination until last.'

She took a clean buff folder from a drawer in the desk, opened it and entered the name 'Julia Young' in the appropriate space.

'We've been trying for this child for ten years,' her client began in a voice now softened with seriousness. 'I had all the infertility tests—Malcolm already had a child by a previous marriage,' she explained quickly. 'I got very upset with all the tests and so did he, especially as there was the extra burden of having to go to the other end of London to have them done so as to protect our privacy a bit. As you're probably aware, Malcolm's something of a celebrity these days, and it would have been very trying if the media had got to know of our situation. They have a way of sympathising which really makes things so much worse,' she smiled as if to apologise for her criticism. 'Anyway, at length we just decided to give up the whole idea of having a child. I thought I was getting too long in the tooth for motherhood and I was thinking how nice it would be to go back to work.

'I was going to apply to one of the university departments of nursing for some sort of research job. You know, there's hardly any grass-roots research into midwifery practice going on at the moment. I thought I'd be able to charm some money out of someone or other . . . and then voilà, a month with no period—and then another! I waited until nine weeks, practically holding my breath, then did one of those commercial tests for us.' She paused.

'And it was positive,' Melanie finished for her.

'Of course, we were thrilled. And then the trouble started,' Julia smiled ruefully. 'I told Malcolm I wanted a home delivery, no unnecessary intervention—the whole bit. He'd always been most sympathetic when we'd discussed natural childbirth before. You know what he's like, how liberal and open over these things. But now it seems things are different. This is our own child.' She frowned momentarily, then added, 'It's true. I don't want to take any unnecessary risks either—obviously.'

'Have you seen a doctor at all?' Melanie enquired gently.

'Yes. I saw my own doctor, a new young man: Toby Robertson.' Melanie noted the name of the same GP who had referred Edna Dupont to the practice. 'He was very good and gave me Bridget Reid's name and address. Malcolm persuaded me to go in to Lessing Lane, and I did so for his sake. But it was just as I'd feared. I saw different midwives on both occasions, and the place was so busy I was dizzy by the time I'd been in the clinic five minutes. Of course, Daniel's a dear—did you know him; Davenport?—and he did his best to make up for all the dematerialising midwives . . . But it was no good. I just told Malcolm in the end that I was coming to see Bridget for the sake of privacy—and here I am.'

Melanie was still recovering from the mention of the consultant who had had charge of Julia's care at Lessing Lane. She checked the fact.

'Yes. He's next in seniority to Malcolm and Malcolm thinks he's a super obstetrician. I don't know about that, but he's certainly a wonderful man.' Julia smiled openly at Melanie, whose stomach seemed to turn over.

'I'm sure he is,' she managed to reply politely. 'Now, have you brought a specimen of urine with you?'

Julia was sixteen weeks pregnant and her weight was trim for her height. Her blood pressure was a normal healthy 130/70 millimetres of mercury and there was nothing in her past medical history that Melanie considered could stand in the way of her having her baby at home. The only thing that concerned Melanie was the question of Julia's age and the increased incidence of Mongolism in babies born to women later in their child-bearing life. But there was a test for this.

'Have you thought about amniocentesis, Julia?' Melanie asked when her client was dressing again.

'Yes, and I don't think I want it,' Julia replied. 'We want this baby so badly,' she explained softly, 'I can't bear even the smallest chance of losing it.'

'The risk is very, very tiny, Julia.'

'Yes, I know.'

'Even taking into account your age?' Melanie persisted gently.

'Even taking that into account!' Julia smiled.

Melanie dropped the subject. Personally, she felt that the risks involved in drawing off a tiny quantity of the fluid which surrounded the baby in the womb were insignificant in comparison with the relief of knowing that your baby was not suffering from spina bifida or Down's syndrome. But she had to respect Julia's choice. Julia, of all people, knew what she was doing in refusing amniocentesis.

'Well, that's about it. Would you like another cup of coffee? You seem to be our only patient this morning.'

'No, thanks, Melanie. I promised I'd meet Malcolm for lunch . . .'

The sound of the front door opening and voices in the hall interrupted them, and Melanie saw Bridget come in with a well-dressed good-looking young man in his early thirties.

'Ah, Melanie, this is Toby Robertson, my tamest young family doctor . . .' began Bridget, then caught sight of Julia.

'Mrs Young!' exclaimed Toby Robertson at the same moment, 'well, hello there! Booking in?'

'Yes, Dr Robertson. I've had a very pleasant morning with Melanie, and I think everything is organised. Oh, Melanie, I forgot to tell you that Dr Robertson asked if he could be present at the birth.'

'Yes, of course,' faltered Melanie. 'It's nice to meet you, Dr Robertson.' She took his hand and met his frankly interested blue-eyed stare.

'It's a pleasure,' he said with emphasis.

Bridget was beaming at everyone. 'Well, I seem to be the only person not to have been introduced to our new client, Melanie . . .'

Julia Young put that immediately to rights, introducing herself. 'And before Melanie tries to corner you behind my back, I might as well tell you that I'm the wife of her ex-boss at Lessing Lane,' she grinned, 'which frightened her half to death at first, but doesn't any more. Isn't that right, Melanie?'

Bridget looked from Melanie to Julia Young and back to Melanie again, keeping a diplomatic silence. 'And where were you two rushing off to?' she asked at last.

'Julia was just leaving, and I wasn't going anywhere,' replied Melanie.

'Toby and I thought we'd pick you up and take you out for a snack lunch,' Bridget told her. 'We bumped heads over my last delivery, and I realised you two hadn't met yet. Why don't we all have lunch together? Are you dashing off anywhere in particular, Mrs Young?'

Julia glanced at her wristwatch. 'Well, I've missed Malcolm now.' She looked up. 'That sounds lovely. Where did you put my coat, Melanie?'

Sitting beside Toby in the old green estate car which had obviously served him faithfully for some years, Melanie quietly observed her new medical colleague. He was very attractive. There were laughter lines at the corners of his blue eyes and above his mouth. His features were mobile and alert and he had the well-scrubbed good looks of the model medical student which he had once undoubtedly been.

'How are you enjoying your new job, Melanie?' he enquired, bestowing a smile upon her warm as summer sun.

'Very much,' replied Melanie easily.

'Well, I hope this working lunch will be the first of many,' he responded.

Melanie smiled. But something inside her saw a warning light and she felt slightly wary of his enthusiasm. There was a very fine line between male friendliness and the suggestion of something else, and it was one to which Melanie was especially sensitive. She glanced into the rearview mirror and caught Bridget's eye, and then her wink.

Toby stopped the car outside a picturesque riverside pub and went round the car opening doors for everyone. He bowed extravagantly for Melanie. 'Real ale and cottage pie within,' he announced.

She was aware of his approving gaze taking in her long legs and the swing of her heather-coloured tweed skirt. He rested momentarily on her waist and then followed the line of her fitting sweater up to her face. She blushed.

'What's wrong, Melanie?' he asked innocently. She coiled a strand of hair nervously around her fingers and pushed it viciously up under a pin. 'Your hair looks smashing.'

'Yes, thank you, Dr Robertson,' she responded with annoyance. 'We'll lose the others . . .' As she stepped forward he put his hand beneath her elbow.

'That wouldn't be so terrible, now would it?' he asked with a sparkle in his eyes.

She told herself off for reacting too seriously to him. He was obviously harmless enough, and she should be able to enjoy his patter. After all, it was a long time since she had met anyone new who had taken such an instant liking to her. She walked beside him into the crowded lunchtime bar, trying to accommodate her vision to the gloom, the smoke and the mass of lunchtime drinkers. Then the crowd thinned and she caught sight of Julia and Bridget. They were standing one on either side of Dr Daniel Davenport at the brass-railed bar.

'Ah, there you are, Melanie. I was just telling Daniel here about our morning!' Julia's eyes were positively dancing with excitement.

Melanie met Dr Davenport's look, and knew instantly why Toby had made her so ill at ease. He was a younger and much less striking version of the man who now stood before her. But there was no softness, no hint of teasing or even humour in the eyes which held hers now. The consultant seemed to have turned momentarily into stone.

'Do you two know one another?' Julia went on chattily, 'This is turning out to be quite a party. What can I order for you, Melanie?'

'I'll get Miss Aarts a drink,' the consultant stated. 'What do you want?'

As he spoke, his eyes travelled down to Melanie's elbow where Toby's hand still rested lightly. She pulled her arm away violently.

'Gin and tonic, please,' she articulated clearly.

'Oh, look, there's a table free over there,' said Bridget. 'Toby, be an angel . . .' Toby Robertson ran and claimed the table, and Julia followed him, carrying a tray of drinks. Melanie was just about to join them when the consultant stopped her.

'I'm leaving now,' he said, handing her the drink he had just bought her, 'but I'd like you to meet me here this evening. Seven-thirty. Is that all right?'

Melanie watched him raise his eyebrows infinitesimally as if to emphasise his request; a request that amounted not so such to an invitation as to an order.

'Yes,' she said without thinking.

'Good,' he responded coldly, and turned and left. The sight of his broad back held her transfixed for a moment, then he was lost in the crowd.

She picked her way carefully towards where the others were, hoping her feelings did not show on her face. Evidently they didn't.

'Come and sit down and tell us all why you left Lessing Lane. We've all been speculating like mad and getting it all wrong, I'm sure.' Toby patted a chair next to him invitingly.

Melanie glanced at Julia, who gave her a candid smile.

'It's okay,' she said, 'don't mind me. I won't report a word you say! Actually, though,' she added, 'Malcolm's all for independent midwifery, you know. He gave a paper on it somewhere . . . to some course or other for midwives. When it comes to his own wife, it's a bit . . . Anyway, it's not Malcolm who reacts badly to things like that, although some of the other senior medical men at Lessing Lane feel a little more strongly about it . . .' She broke off, as if she had already said too much.

Melanie's heart lurched.

'It's our job to educate them,' said Bridget, digging Toby in the ribs with a friendly grin. 'Isn't that right, Dr Robertson?'

'Certainly,' agreed Toby. 'Everybody isn't as enlightened as we might wish. Yet.' He shook his head as much as to express his despair at the ignorance of his own profession.

'I drink to that,' said Julia Young. 'Where are those sandwiches I ordered? I'm ravenous!'

'Eating for two . . .' chorused Bridget and Melanie in unison, then stopped short.

'Well,' said Toby, 'there's an unenlightened outlook, if ever I heard one!'

Everybody laughed.

If the morning had been unusually calm, the afternoon made up for it. Melanie and Bridget saw twenty antenatal clients between them before five o'clock, then the telephone summoned them to a delivery.

'I'll go,' Melanie said, rapidly filling in the notes of the last client she had seen.

She grabbed a set of equipment, leaving the other identical set for Bridget should she be called out too. Bridget pushed a set of case notes into Melanie's hand.

'Thanks a lot, Melanie. Whew, this'll teach us to take nice relaxed liquid lunches! See you later, or tomorrow.'

As she passed the waiting room, Melanie noticed that there were still three more women to be seen. It was good to get out into the fresh air, and Melanie looked forward to the delivery with her usual mixture of poignant pleasure and anxiety that all should go well.

It did go well, and two hours later she was behind the wheel of her car again, the cries of the newborn baby boy still ringing in her ears. She felt elated, as always after a delivery, especially after one that had gone so quickly and smoothly. It was always a wonderful honour to be present at a birth, each one a miracle so different from the last. At moments such as this, Melanie knew she would swap places with nobody in the world and that midwifery was truly her vocation.

The smell of the river wafted in through the open side window of the car, bringing her suddenly and sharply down to earth. What on earth was the time? What was she thinking about? She was supposed to meet Daniel Davenport at half past seven and now there was barely time to get to the pub in time, let alone to wash and change.

She swiftly took her bearings, reversed into a side street and headed back towards the river. The gleaming white Porsche was already there, alone, facing out over the quietly flowing river like a seagull. Melanie parked beside the white car, remembering her former impression of its feline qualities. She tutted to herself. I'm nearly as confused about the car as by the man, she thought. She tried to collect herself as she walked towards the pub, wishing it was not so late, that she'd had time to go home and change.

Daniel Davenport sat in a far corner of the almost empty bar, an untouched pint of beer on the table in front of him. He was gazing out over the river and did not see Melanie come into the bar. As she joined him, she watched his eyes guard themselves. What do I do to have that effect on him? she thought. She felt sapped of all the strength and joy that had filled her only a short time ago.

'What do you want?' he asked for the second time that day.

Melanie cleared her throat nervously.

'I'd like a fresh orange juice,' she answered him.

'No gin this evening?' he asked scathingly.

'No. An orange juice would be very nice,' she responded.

He stood up, his strong build emphasised by the well-cut casual clothes he wore. Melanie had never noticed what he wore before. She had always seen him in a white coat, until this lunchtime . . . it was oddly disconcerting to be alone with him here this evening. She struggled to compose herself for whatever was to come.

He put the orange juice down in front of her and resumed his place opposite.

'I want to speak to you about Julia Young,' he said.

It was what she had feared. Melanie tried to get the ethics of her situation straight inside her head. But she couldn't; everything seemed so confused. Everything had happened so quickly. She had had no time to adjust to the fact that Julia Young was her patient, let alone to digest the truth of the strange position it put them both in with regard to Professor Young and Daniel Davenport.

Julia had been perfectly frank about everything, but it would take all Melanie's willpower to control this interview with her ex-consultant, especially as she herself was so unprepared to fight with him.

'I don't really want to . . . I don't really think we should discuss Mrs Young . . .' she stammered.

He threw her a furious glance, then took a long draught of his beer.

'Listen, Miss Aarts. I don't need you or anyone else to tell me my ethical position, or yours, over Mrs Young. And I have no intention of discussing her . . . her case, that is, with you.'

Melanie took a sip of cool juice, which she then found herself unable to swallow. He was talking as though he considered it a waste of time to discuss patient care with her, not because the case involved was that of Julia Young, but because one as lowly as she, Melanie, could have nothing useful to contribute to such a discussion. She swallowed hard.

'Good,' she said.

'I just want to make clear to you the magnitude of your responsibility as a . . . ' he sighed insolently, 'a "free" practitioner. It's very great indeed.'

'I'm aware of that,' said Melanie quietly. Suddenly the expression upon her client's face when she had handed her her baby an hour or so before returned to her with great clarity. 'Thank you for your . . . concern,' she added.

Daniel Davenport fixed her icily.

'I'm sure that you are very . . . able,' he said, with obvious lack of conviction, 'both of you.'

If Melanie could take insults herself, she was not going to accept them on behalf of her new colleague.

'Bridget is a wonderful midwife,' she declared coldly, 'but she doesn't need a vote of confidence from you. I don't know why you asked me to meet you tonight. If it was just to talk about one of my patients—well, I think you should know better. If it was simply to insult me professionally, I wish you hadn't bothered. I've never been in any doubt as to your opinion of my professional competence, ever since our first encounter at Lessing Lane,' she flung at him.

He winced, then watched her face steadily for a minute. He swallowed the last of his beer.

'I'm having another one of those,' he said. 'Will you join me?'

'No, thank you,' replied Melanie coldly, 'I haven't eaten yet, and I'd like to do so soon.'

Her companion hesitated briefly, stood up, then sat down again. Melanie thought she detected a slight softening in his features.

'It wasn't too pleasant in here at lunchtime,' he said.

'It was terrible,' she agreed.

'Who was the young chap?'

Melanie finished her juice.

'Mrs Young's GP,' she said.

'Know him well?' the consultant asked casually.

Melanie was both puzzled by his question and surprised by the change in Dr Davenport. He seemed almost to be trying to placate her.

'No,' she answered truthfully, 'I only met him for the first time today.'

She sat in silence and they looked at one another. He seemed to know that he could hold her attention like this for as long as it suited him. She was irritated and fascinated by his composure, his power over her.

'I'll run you home,' he offered lightly.

'No need,' she said, 'I've got my own car outside.'

They left the bar and walked towards the river wall where their two cars stood side by side.

'Very cosy,' he said sarcastically as the sight of the two lonely vehicles.

'Yours isn't a very cosy type of car,' she remarked, 'more cobra-like than cosy.' There I go again, she thought.

'Yes, she's a beauty, isn't she?' Was it only in her imagination that he underlined the gender? 'I had a bit of a tiff with a tree before I came up to London and the garage only delivered her back into my hands last month. I'd missed her. They did a good job patching her up, and drove her up from Elchester for me—very decent of them. Let me think now, I'm sure I got her back the afternoon we did the ultra-sound on your redheaded lady—Mrs Dupont, wasn't it?'

Melanie could not hide her surprise. She hoped his memory accounted for it to him.

'Okay—well, goodbye for now, Miss Aarts.'

Melanie filed away the ghost of a half-smile he gave her. It might have to last her a long time. She drove to Bedford Park through the early dark realising that she was lightheaded with hunger.

Rachel was out when she got into the flat. She cooked herself an omelette and some green beans and got herself a glass of milk. What was he doing now? She admitted to herself that she had been stupidly pleased about the car. It was silly of her to feel so relieved; after all, it was hardly concrete evidence upon which to support the belief that he had no wife.

Nevertheless, she felt ridiculously pleased. She could not get over the feeling that the consultant had had his anger appeased this evening and had backed off from the lecture that he had planned for her. She could not think how she had effected this, but she had the distinct impression that she had won a tactical victory. It was some small solace for the fact that she would probably not see him again for some time, if at all.

CHAPTER THREE

THE worst thing about having Julia Young as her first full patient was that Melanie couldn't talk about it with anybody outside the practice. If this client had been anyone else, she would at least have been able to share her pleasure and worries with Rachel. But as things were, she was bound by all the laws of personal and professional confidentiality not to discuss Julia's case with anyone who knew her or her husband.

As the weeks went by, so her secret worry increased, and at last she found she had to speak to Bridget about it.

'I saw Julia today,' she began as they sat down to a cup of coffee after the last of their ante-natal patients had left.

'Yes?' responded Bridget. 'How is she?'

'She's fine. Everything's going like clockwork.' Melanie touched the wooden table, then tapped her own head with a quick smile. 'I just hope it continues like this.'

'And what makes you think it might not?'

'Oh, I don't know,' Melanie shrugged.

'It's that famous husband of hers, isn't it? Putting the wind up you.'

'Well, not exactly him . . .' To her amazement the whole story of her meeting with Daniel Davenport came pouring out of Melanie. 'It was as if he drained me of all my hard-won confidence,' she said when she had told Bridget everything he had said. 'He made me feel as if such an important patient and such a precious pregnancy couldn't and shouldn't be left in the hands of one as lowly as I—a mere midwife. Still, I gave as good as I got,' she added, 'but since—well, it's just been really getting to me, Bridget.' She felt close to tears. 'I'm sorry.'

'Listen, Julia believes in you, doesn't she?' Bridget replied firmly but gently.

'She seems to—completely. I mean, unless she's just being polite.'

'Is she the type to be polite? She struck me as a pretty forceful lady who knew what she wanted and said so.'

Melanie knew this was completely true. How could that man do this to her? Her whole vision was distorted by what he had said one evening over a drink.

'Melanie, this is ridiculous,' Bridget was continuing. 'I don't know what this Davenport man has said to you, but he had no right to do so. Melanie, you don't need to be reminded of your professional responsibilities by anyone. You know as well as I do that *every* patient is important and *every* pregnancy precious.'

Melanie nodded miserably.

'Listen, who *is* that man? What is there between you two? I'm sorry to have to speak to you about something that seems so personal, but he was as charming as a man could be before you arrived on the scene the other lunchtime, and like a bear with a sore head the next minute. I couldn't help noticing,' Bridget finished apologetically.

In spite of their increasingly close working relationship Bridget and Melanie still knew very little about one another's private lives. After the gossip and intrigue of life at Lessing Lane, Melanie had found her new circumstances beautifully refreshing, but now she felt an overwhelming desire to confide further and to have the benefit of Bridget's sound advice.

'I don't know anything about him really,' Melanie began carefully. 'He came to Lessing Lane about six months ago from the West Country. I think he's married, or newly divorced. Anyway, ever since we first met on the wards we've been finding ways to drive one another crazy. He's a good obstetrician—the Prof.'s blue-eyed boy, actually—and I used to think I was a pretty reasonable midwife. But he seems to have the capacity to make me look and feel like an incompetent pupil of nineteen.' She swallowed hard. She found she was half smiling by the time she had finished this summation of the situation between herself and the consultant.

Bridget joined her. 'Oh, yes,' she almost grinned, 'I think I get the picture. But,' she added seriously, 'Melanie, you really mustn't let him undermine you. Good grief, I wouldn't have asked you to be my partner if you'd been a mediocre midwife. I gave the post to somebody who I thought excelled . . .'

'Thank you, Bridget,' Melanie cut in, embarrassed, 'I'm so glad I talked to you. It was really getting to me.'

'I'm glad you did too. Now, there's a client whom I saw today in whom I'd like you to take a special interest.'

Bridget unearthed some notes from the pile on the table in front of them, and Melanie had a second in which to collect herself before she opened them and glanced through the introductory notes.

'She's a lovely Indian lady, Amina Chowdhary,' said Bridget, 'and she's very appreciative of our brand of care. It's against her religion to be examined by a male doctor, so she wants to avoid hospitals if she possibly can . . .'

The telephone interrupted her.

'I'll get it, Melanie, it's probably Stephen wondering if I'm coming home tonight!'

Bridget's husband hardly ever rang her at the practice. For the first time, Melanie realised that her partner hardly ever spoke about him and that when she did the closeness and trust of their relationship was evident. For a second she found herself watching Bridget with wistful envy.

'It's for you. Joe . . . Peters?'

Melanie took the receiver with surprise.

'Hello? Melanie? Good. I was afraid I might have missed you. Look, how about that jar this evening? I've just been doing an ultra-sound and remembered the last one I did. It's ages since I said I'd call you—been busy, I'm afraid. Well, how about it?'

'I'd love to meet you, Joe,' Melanie answered. 'I'd

like to just go back to the flat first and tidy up . . .'

'Oh, never mind about that. I'll see you at The Foresters about six, and we'll have something to eat together later, okay?'

Well, it was only Joe, after all. She didn't have to dress up for her old friend.

'Okay, fine. I'll see you around six.'

She hung up. Still, it was just as well that she worked in mufti these days. Her social life seemed to be picking up no end.

'Well,' said Bridget lightly, 'this little lot will wait until tomorrow. I think I'll go home to my husband and cook us a candlelit supper—or eat the one he's cooked me!' She flashed Melanie her quick, shy smile—the one she'd seen before in the same context.

'That sounds nice,' said Melanie.

'It usually is!' her partner replied, picking up the empty cups from the table, 'And you'd better be off too, or you'll be late for your date.' She winked at Melanie. 'Have a lovely time yourself.

Melanie went straight into the ladies' room in the saloon bar of the pub next to the South-West City Hospital. She took her hair down and combed it, then left it loose. She felt quite fresh, considering the day behind her, and lighter-spirited since she had confided in Bridget. Her grey skirt and red and grey striped jersey were comfortable and suitable for the evening ahead. She only had to rid herself of this stupid yearning for a different partner to share it with.

It was now more than a month since her meeting with Daniel Davenport and, of course, she had not seen him since. It was odd that Joe should have phoned her today, just when she had at last decided to unburden herself about that other meeting. Telling Bridget had made her realise just how much it had affected her, and she could not help almost wishing she had refused Joe's invitation.

But when he walked into the pub, one glance at his open, friendly smile set her at her ease. He was so obviously glad to see her, and she felt flooded with her old affection for him. All the times he had championed her, complimented her upon her part in a difficult delivery and shared her disappointment in a professional failure came back to her.

'Our first date,' he beamed. 'Nice to see you, Melanie.' He kissed the back of her hand gallantly.

Melanie found a table and waited for Joe to bring their drinks. She remembered how sorry she had been to have to miss the Christmas Party at Lessing Lane when the 'flu epidemic finally caught up with her and laid her low —the last of the labour wing staff to succumb.

'Thanks, Joe.' She supped her half pint of beer and pulled open the packet of crisps he'd brought her. 'I'm starving!'

'That's not supper,' Joe promised. 'We could go to that new Greek place in the High Road.'

'Later, Joe. I'll survive. How are you?'

Dr Peters grimaced at her over his glasses. 'Suffering from intransigent consultant disease,' he whispered conspiringly.

Melanie giggled. 'Is it as bad as that?'

'Worse. The other day I had the impudence to suggest that an eight-foot-high eighteen-year-old prima gravida might just manage to deliver without help from his scissors and he nearly used them on me instead. Uggh!'

He faked self-defence.

'Oh, Joe, you're good for me. I miss you,' Melanie smiled.

'That's two of us. I mean, I miss you too.' Joe sipped his lager. 'What's your new partner like?'

'Great,' answered Melanie, 'she's amazingly calm and competent and in control and generally good for me too.'

'You're all those things yourself,' Joe rejoined loyally, 'so how is she good for you?'

'Well, you know, she makes me trust myself, and that's so important when you're working out from beneath the protective wing of a hospital.'

'I can imagine,' said Joe sincerely. 'But are you enjoying yourself? Really?'

'I really am. It's a whole new world, Joe. I'm sure it was the right move for me.'

'So am I.' Joe's face was serious. 'You know, I think it's really important for women to be able to choose for themselves a midwife and a home delivery if they want it and there's no medical reason against them.'

Melanie nodded, appreciating once again her ex-colleague's support. It was not that medical support for her profession was particularly lacking; it was just that the quality of that encouragement seemed sometimes to lack enthusiasm.

'Would you like to come and watch us working, Joe?' she asked, suddenly keen to repay his generosity. 'I could ask Bridget if you could come to a home delivery. Then you could see what I mean about her.'

'That would be amazing! Could you really arrange that Melanie?'

'I don't see why not. If we can get one of our clients to agree to an extra audience of one,' she replied.

'Well, if you can, I'd love to come along,' Joe responded. 'Hey, isn't it about time we ate?'

They drained their glasses and stood up. Melanie vaguely recognised several of the people sitting nearby. The Foresters served as a local for the staff who worked at the SWCH. For some reason, the established staff at Lessing Lane preferred another place; a little-used pub at the far end of the Lane which they shared with one or two trusty old tramps who lived in a squat nearby. She had remembered this when Joe had asked her to meet him tonight, confident that she would be unlikely to meet anyone she knew from the maternity annexe.

'Good evening, sir.'

Melanie stepped out on to the pavement behind Joe, wondering whom he had greeted so formally. It was Daniel Davenport. The subject of their earlier amusement was evidently less than pleased to see them. He barely grunted in response to Joe's polite acknowledgement of him and narrowed his eyes at Melanie.

'Good evening to you!' The travesty of a courtesy was directed at her. 'Miss Aarts and Dr Peters! Well, have a pleasant one.'

He excused himself and plunged into the bar as if he could not rid himself soon enough of their presence.

Joe looked at Melanie and shrugged.

'What did we do?' he asked.

'*I* don't have to *do* anything,' she responded, half in anger and half in despair.

'Oh, well,' retorted her companion, 'let's see if a bottle of Retsina restores our flagging spirits!'

And he marched her off in the direction of the restaurant.

'It's the spring rush,' announced Bridget grimly as she set out for her second delivery of the morning.

Melanie had seen hardly anything of her for the past couple of weeks and babies seemed to be arriving at an alarming rate. It was March already, and Melanie recalled once more that this month, along with April and September was a peak arrival time.

But, facing a waiting room full of ante-natal clients alone, she knew she was not sorry to be busy at the practice. It kept her mind off her private life, which seemed to be emptier than it had ever been. A communication gap seemed to have opened up between herself and Rachel since had she left Lessing Lane. Rachel's shifts kept her away from the flat for long hours—a fact which Melanie had never noticed when she was working them too. Between Rachel's shifts and her own heavy on-call commitment, the two midwives hardly ever saw each other at home these days.

And as for a social life, it was non-existent. Melanie admitted to herself. The evening out with Joe had been fun, but he had not rung her since. He was busy at Lessing Lane with the same 'spring rush' which was occupying Bridget and herself, she knew, but still, she couldn't help wishing he would call. Toby Robertson was a fairly regular visitor to the practice, but his over-enthusiastic, boyish attention grated on her.

She put her head around the waiting-room door.

'Next?'

Mrs Edna Dupont heaved herself up out of her chair and replaced the copy of *Woman's Own* which she had been reading. As she stood up she winced, then her face relaxed and she straightened her back. She was hugely pregnant and her back had been sore for a week or more, a sign which Melanie hoped indicated that delivery was imminent.

She tested Mrs Dupont's urine, weighed her and measured her blood pressure. Satisfied that all the routine tests were normal, she asked Edna to climb up on to the examination couch so that she could palpate her abdomen.

'It won't be long now,' her client assured her. 'I'm getting those cramps all the time now.'

'Braxton Hicks' contractions,' Melanie murmured. She could feel the baby easily, its head already fully engaged in the pelvis ready for birth.

'When did you feel the baby's head drop down, Edna?' she asked.

'Just after I left here last week,' Edna answered. 'I've been that uncomfortable since! But I knew what it was from the last one, so I didn't bother to let you know.'

'I should have come to you today,' Melanie told her. 'I'm so sorry you've come all this way on the bus at this late stage for you.'

'Oh, don't worry about that, dear. It's no trouble. But I'm sure it won't be long now.'

Melanie helped Edna swing her legs down off the couch, noting the very slight swelling around her ankles. But her BP was within normal limits and there had been no protein in her urine. Suddenly Melanie remembered what Bridget had said just before she left this morning.

'Edna,' she said, 'we've a favour to ask of you. You know the dark-haired doctor whom we met at the hospital when you had your sound test done?'

'Yes . . .' replied Edna uncertainly. Then, 'Oh, yes, that nice one with the glasses?'

'That's right—Dr Peters. Well, he'd very much like to come and watch while your baby's being born. Would you mind that very much?'

'Not a bit, dear,' Edna responded cheerfully, 'it'll be quite a party. My first one says she's going to watch, even if she has to miss play school!'

'Oh, that's lovely. Dr Peters will be pleased. Thank you, Edna. And I expect we'll be seeing you very soon.'

She helped Mrs Dupont on with her coat, making a mental note to telephone Lessing Lane and warn Joe that his home delivery was on the cards for tonight.

But the last of her ante-natal clients had hardly gone out of the front door when the telephone summoned her and Edna's husband informed her that the waters had broken. Edna was apparently calm and managing the first stage of her labour happily, but things were moving quite quickly.

Melanie rang Lessing Lane, cursing the slowness of the busy switchboard. Joe was still seeing ante-natal patients himself. He took Edna's address and promised to get there as soon as he possibly could.

When Melanie arrived at Edna's cosy terraced house she found her client resting on her bed, her husband sitting beside her and faithfully breathing with her through the pains. These were coming every five minutes now, and Melanie prepared to do an internal examination to determine how dilated the cervix was. She asked Edna's husband to leave the bedroom and smiled at her.

'How's it going?' she asked the moment they were alone.

'Fine, Sister. I think it's easier this time round. Or could that be my imagination? Oooh!'

Melanie counted slowly to thirty, waiting for the contraction to pass. As Edna's face relaxed so too did the tension over her abdomen beneath Melanie's hand.

'Well, the longest part is over, Edna,' she said after

she had finished examining her, 'the neck of the womb is already half open.'

Mr Dupont reappeared with two cups of tea: one for himself and one for Melanie.

'Milk but no sugar, please,' she said. 'How are you feeling, Mr Dupont?'

'A bit nervous,' he admitted, pushing back a lock of hair as red as that of his wife, 'but I'm glad she's here and we're both in it together.'

He was so obviously pleased to have Melanie in the house at last that she had to smile.

'Edna's doing a super job,' she told him. 'Why don't you have your tea next door, take a break? I'll stay here and chat with your wife.'

He kissed his wife lightly on the forehead. 'I'll slip next door then, love, and see what Janice's up to.' He threw Melanie a relieved glance. 'My little girl's next door with her granny,' he explained.

'It's harder for him than for me,' said Edna, her face screwing up again, 'I mean . . . I've got work to do.'

The pains rapidly increased in strength and duration until Melanie could feel them over the entire abdomen and she guessed that the cervix was fully dilated.

She was just completing her second internal examination, having checked the baby's strong heartbeat, when she heard Mr Dupont answer the front door bell and Joe's voice in the hall downstairs.

'Here's your favourite doctor, Edna!' she said, and a couple of seconds later Joe's head appeared around the bedroom door.

'Not too late, am I?'

Edna managed a smile. 'Nearly, Doctor,' she puffed. 'Oh, I do feel sick!'

Melanie knew that this common sign marked progress from first into second stage of labour, and she prepared to guide her client's desire to bear down.

The next twenty minutes passed very quickly. Mr Dupont and his four-year-old daughter came and stood quietly in the corner of the room together while Melanie and Joe worked together to help Edna to maintain a comfortable and optimal position. At last the baby's head and shoulders were delivered and Melanie grasped the child, helping it to emerge finally into the world.

'You've got a little boy, Edna!' she announced.

Edna propped herself up on one elbow to look at her son, then lay back on the pillows, tears in her eyes. Her little girl and husband came and kissed her, and Joe gave Melanie a hand to tidy things up at the other end of the bed. She waited until the cord had stopped pulsating, took a sample of blood from it, then tied and cut it. After the preliminary Apgar scores had been assessed, she wrapped baby Dupont in a clean towel and handed him to his mother.

'He's very little,' announced a small clear voice, and everybody looked at the proud new sister. 'When will he be able to play with me?'

Edna laughed and put her free arm around her daughter. Happiness, relief and release of all the tension of the past few hours flowed from them all.

'There's a lot to be said for home delivery,' said Joe in a quiet aside to Melanie.

She was exhausted by the time they emerged from the house some two hours later, but glad that Joe had stayed to help and watch the whole thing from start to finish. They pulled their coats around them as the brisk evening breeze met them, glad of the warmth from the tot of Mr Dupont's best whisky which he had insisted upon their accepting.

'How about something to eat?' suggested Joe.

They drove their own cars to the same Greek restaurant they had been to before, and easily found parking space in front of it.

'Kebabs for me again, I think,' said Melanie once they had found a table, 'they were super last time.'

Joe ordered, then lifted his glass of wine to hers. 'Here's to my favourite midwife!' he saluted her.

She enjoyed her meal. It was nice to sip the resiny wine and to feel herself relaxing over a pleasant meal in

the company of somebody to whom she could freely
talk. Joe was such easy and amusing company. Even in
her tired state he could make her laugh, and did so
several times before they found themselves sipping their
thick, sweet Turkish coffee.

'That was lovely—thank you, Joe. But I wish you'd let
me pay for myself. You don't have to impress me, you
know, or treat me like some special date.' She said it
lightly enough, while he slipped her coat around her
shoulders, and was surprised at the frown on his face
when she caught sight of him again.

Outside, she expected him to wave his usual cheery
goodbye and make for his car, but instead he seemed to
hesitate. He hovered for a moment in the darkened
street, the swaying bare branches of the trees throwing
strange shadows across his face. Then he caught her in
his arms. Melanie was so shocked by his unexpected
action that for a moment she was powerless to break
free.

He kissed her with none of the gentleness or humour
for which she had always liked him. He seemed oblivious
to her for what seemed an age, then seemed to realise
her shock and drew away, embarrassment and hurt in
his eyes.

'I'm sorry, Melanie. I didn't mean . . . I didn't mean
to . . .'

'It's all right, Joe,' Melanie whispered, passing her
hand involuntarily across her mouth. 'I was just . . .
surprised, that's all.'

'Damn it,' muttered Joe, then his voice cleared. 'I'm
sorry, Melanie. Look, can we forget that that ever
happened?'

'Yes,' Melanie replied, 'of course we can. Good night,
Joe, and thanks again for the meal.'

She almost ran to her car and pushed her key trem-
blingly into the ignition. It was one thing to know how to
handle a situation in an adult way, and another to
control your own emotional response to it. It was one
thing to tell somebody that you forgave them, and

another to erase the memory of that pressure on your lips, the taste of wine, that tightening embrace. Until tonight she had enjoyed Joe's friendship quite unselfconsciously. It had never occurred to her that he could treat her like . . . that. Anger took the place of shock inside her. Why couldn't she have a simple friendship with him? Damn it, he was right—damn, damn it!

'. . . and then he kissed me. I couldn't believe it! I was furious!' stated Melanie. She cleaned the top of a trolley with spirit. She had told Bridget the story of Edna's delivery.

'You know what your trouble is? You're exhausted.'

Melanie looked at her partner in stunned amazement. 'And what about *you*?' she returned.

'I'm used to it.'

The two midwives had seen thirty clients that day between them, and attended three deliveries in the past twenty-four hours.

'When did you last take a full day off?' Bridget persisted.

'Two weeks ago,' admitted Melanie.

'Ridiculous!' Bridget exploded.

She shut the door firmly on the newly cleaned consulting room and drew Melanie into the coffee room. The late afternoon sunshine filtered in through the white voile curtains and some thrushes and a robin redbreast hunted for worms among the late crocuses in the borders outside.

Melanie took the piece of paper Bridget handed her without really looking at it. It seemed to be a programme of some sort.

'What's this?' she asked absentmindedly.

'Look at it. I was going to go myself, but I think it'll do you more good. You've worked very hard since you joined me and you need a break and some outside encouragement. I haven't mentioned it before, because I didn't think I'd have time to go after all—but I think now we should just make time for you.'

The programme was for a three-day conference on advances in delivery techniques, to be held in The Hague in Holland, beginning the next morning.

'But you have to register at eleven tomorrow morning . . .' Melanie began in amazement, 'and who'll help you?' Her head was teeming. Among all the names of eminent doctors who were to address the meeting was that of her aunt Ineke, who was listed as President of the Dutch Association of Professional Midwives—a title of which Melanie knew nothing!

'Get a plane,' Bridget was saying matter-of-factly. 'You'll have plenty of time to go there in the morning. I'll ring Heathrow and Gatwick to see which flight gets you to Schiphol Airport at nine. There are always lots of businessmen's flights. And don't worry about the practice—that's my job. I'll get a locum.' Smiling at Melanie's guilty frown, she added, 'Go on! It's an investment for the practice to have you better educated and right up to date.'

'Oh, Bridget . . . it's amazing!' Melanie managed.

The rest of the day passed before she had time to worry any more. She had soon booked herself aboard a plane from Heathrow, leaving at eight the following morning. There was a last-minute panic at Bedford Park when she couldn't find her passport, but she discovered it at last hiding in a clothes drawer, and fell into bed too tired to do anything but sleep soundly until her alarm roused her at six.

Rachel was in the kitchen making breakfast before going in for an early shift at Lessing Lane when Melanie finally appeared. She was astonished to see Melanie dressed up in red cord trousers, red shirt and thick natural-coloured jacket—all things which she had brought newly with her first pay packet from her new job, and not for work.

'What are you doing togged up to the nines?' she asked.

'Going off to The Hague for a conference,' Melanie said happily. She had taken time dressing, adding red bracelets and making sure that her hair was beautifully neatly secured at the nape of her neck. She knew she looked good, and it made her feel confident.

Rachel's eyes opened wide.

'You're joking!'

'No,' said Melanie. 'I'm not taking a coat,' she prompted.

Rachel looked her flatmate up and down.

'You look fantastic,' she said. 'You lucky thing!'

'Thank you, Rachel. Actually, I'm really excited. My aunt is speaking at the conference, and guess what? She's been made President to the Dutch Midwives' Association, and she didn't even tell me! So it's a surprise for her and one for me too.'

'I've not noticed it before, but I really think this new job of yours is doing you good, Mella,' said Rachel, thoughtfully taking a bite of toast.

'Well, we could always start up in practice together . . .'

'No!' responded Rachel vehemently, her mouth full. 'I'm not *that* sure you've done the right thing. Yet!'

Melanie walked briskly to Turnham Green and caught the tube straight through to Heathrow Airport. It was a glorious spring day. The train sped through the stations thronged with commuters and the sun gilded the neat suburban streets so that they seemed to awake from winter and make ready for a new year.

It was lovely to be off like this, whisked out of routine before she had time to worry about anything and with the special magic of springtime in Holland lying in wait for her. Melanie jumped off the train at the terminal and took her place among the smart businessmen and women on the travelator. The silver corridors of the great airport seemed to lead her into a different world.

It was a world of palm trees and sun, of beautiful suntanned people, strange exotic destinations and lovely cool uniformed girls who moved themselves as smoothly as jet planes. Melanie was enchanted by the calm busy atmosphere of the huge terminal building where she found the Royal Dutch Airlines desk and checked in exactly an hour before her flight was called. All she had to do now was to buy some gulders at the bank in the terminal concourse.

This done, she wandered about happily, enjoying her freedom until the announcement over the tannoy which summoned her to gate number three for embarkation. The small silver and turquoise jet filled up quickly. Melanie found her own seat next to a window and looked out at the runway which awaited them. She always found these last moments before departure thrilling. She loved flying: the exhilaration of take-off and the beauty of the patchwork land as it appeared and disappeared beneath the clouds.

'Well, well. Good morning, Miss Aarts. Fancy meeting you here!'

Daniel Davenport greeted her coolly, took off and neatly folded his raincoat before stowing it above her in the luggage rack, and eased himself carefully into the seat next to her.

She caught a fleeting whiff of his aftershave and was powerfully aware of her usual unfailing inner response to this man's presence. At the same time she had a sense of unreality, so far had her everyday working life been from her thoughts. It was as if she had dreamed his arrival, but she heard herself say good morning.

'You don't seem to be very pleased to see me,' the consultant remarked amiably. 'And I thought you'd be glad of company when I glimpsed your name on the passenger list. I even changed my own seat . . .'

'Oh, I am glad . . .' she said, flustered, 'it's just that it's rather a surprise, that's all.'

'A surprise?' he queried, eyebrows raised.

'Yes.'

'You seem very nervous this morning, Miss Aarts. Are you afraid of flying?'

Melanie looked fully for the first time that morning into the face of the man sitting next to her. She saw the slight lift of his eyebrows and was reminded of the last time he had looked at her like this. The arrogant condescension with which he had treated her at their last meeting swiftly superimposed itself on this new situation, and she felt anger flutter in her stomach.

'No,' she stated, with eyes flashing, 'I am not afraid of flying, Dr Davenport—not in the least. As a matter of fact, I like it very much.'

'Do you now?'

She watched with mounting irritation a muscle twitch in his cheek as a half-smile appeared on his face. She did not see any reason for him to mock her words.

'Why do you delight in upsetting me, Dr Davenport?' she asked icily.

'I don't, Miss Aarts. It's just that you're so easily upset. The moment that we're airborne, though, I shall buy you a gin and tonic to make up for my bad behaviour.'

Melanie relaxed her guard. She knew there was at least some truth in what he said: she was ridiculously over-sensitive to him.

'It's much too early in the morning for that,' she smiled.

The plane taxied away from the terminal building and out towards the tarmac.

'I suppose you're going to this jamboree in The Hague too?' he asked casually, just as the plane lifted off the ground.

'Yes.' As the plane rose, Melanie's own heart sank. How on earth would she be able to relax and enjoy herself for an instant in Holland with him there too? She cursed herself for her lack of self-possession. She had already considered the possibility that she would be completely outnumbered at this conference by arrogant male obstetricians. Well, here was just one more.

'We all have to learn, I suppose,' Dr Davenport commented lazily. He undid his seatbelt and summoned the stewardess with his eyes.

Melanie glanced furiously at his impassive profile.

'And just what's that suppose to mean?' she demanded.

'That we all have to learn,' he repeated blandly. 'Two coffees, please.' The blonde stewardess gave him a scintillating smile which he acknowledged with one of his own. 'I suppose you'll be telling me next that this woman Aarts, the President of the Dutch Midwives, is a relative of yours?' he went on, proffering a copy of the conference programme for Melanie's perusal.

She ignored it.

'Yes, actually, she is. She's my aunt,' she said quietly and deliberately.

The man next to her put his hand over hers in her lap, and she froze, all her attention focused upon the heavy warmth of his touch.

'All right, Melanie,' he said softly, 'don't take me so seriously always.'

She faced him, feeling with horror the tears that had gathered behind her eyelids. The words that had formed in her mind would not come out.

'We might as well call a truce for the duration of the trip,' he continued, 'it's pretty silly to travel separately, for a start.'

Melanie was still absorbing his use of her first name.

'Yes, I suppose it is,' she responded.

Still, she was filled with relief to see the huge flag-fronted building of the Congresgebouw in The Hague at last and to know that the strain of being in Dr Davenport's sole company would soon be over for her. They had found their way easily enough on the unfamiliar train, metro and bus systems from Schiphol to The Hague, Hollandspoor, and then had caught a tram to their final destination. Dr Davenport had been the brisk, matter-of-fact, slightly sardonic character that she remembered only too well from her clinical experience of him at Lessing Lane. It was curiously painful to be so reminded. By the time they reached the Congresgebouw she found it hard to recall the brief moment of intimacy between them on the plane.

'So here we are,' he announced.

Melanie had to admit that she had been glad of his company from the point of view of finding the place. They had arrived at exactly ten to eleven, thanks mainly to the hour time difference between here and London, and in part to his skilful navigation of the foreign transport networks.

'Thank you for your help in getting us here on time,' she said. She was rewarded with a quick half-smile.

'Shame about the company, eh?' he said.

'Okay, thank you for your company too,' Melanie sighed, and smiled at the same time. She felt suddenly very manic about something—the few days ahead. She breathed in the faintly salty air and noticed how much greener everything was here than it had been in London. The air too was warmer and soft. She was glad that she had not encumbered herself with a coat. They walked briskly from the tram stop towards the main entrance of the conference hall and entered the huge reception hall. A large oval reception desk faced them, crowded with people registering their presence at the conference with the clerks. As Melanie had feared, the men— presumably mostly medical men—greatly outnumbered the women, and she felt slightly intimidated by the grandeur of her new surroundings.

'I think I'll go and find a cup of coffee or something until the crowd thins,' she said with more confidence than she felt. There must be some midwives here besides herself, she thought. Surely she would be able to find someone to talk to? She caught sight of one or two distinguished-looking elderly women on her way to the coffee shop, and assumed that they were doctors too. She found herself staring at people's badges as they passed her. She knew there were many male midwives in Holland; it could only be a matter of time before she met somebody from her own profession.

She bought herself a cup of strong black coffee and found a quiet corner in which to drink it. She would have to remember to give Bridget's name when she registered

so that she could take her bedroom at the conference
hotel nearby. Surely fate could not have been so unkind
as to give Daniel Davenport a room next to her there as
well! She found the speculation very uncomfortable and
quickly dismissed it. She finished her coffee and, re-
freshed, wandered around the exhibition stands nearby
before going back downstairs to register.

She need not have worried about being thrown into
contact with Daniel Davenport again. She saw nothing
of him at all for the remainder of the day. But she did
meet a contingent of midwives from Scotland who had
arrived late due to a delay in the departure of their flight
from Glasgow, and with whom she struck up easy
friendship.

After four speakers during the afternoon, each of
whom demanded her whole attention, Melanie was glad
to seek the peace and privacy of her hotel room. Once
there she telephoned her aunt. They planned their
meeting on the last day of the conference, and Ineke
modestly dismissed Melanie's effusive congratulations
on her elevated position in the professional organisation
of which she was President.

'It is only a small country here—it is not such a big
honour. I think you should meet your cousin Jan while
you are here. Did you know that he is now a medical
student at Leiden University?'

'Already?' gasped Melanie.

Her aunt laughed. 'I think you will not recognise your
shy young cousin,' she said. 'That will be a nice surprise
for you. I shall tell him to pick you up tomorrow after the
afternoon session.'

Melanie had last seen her aunt and Jan five years
before, when her fifteen-year-old cousin had been less
than interested in talking to his much older English
cousin.

The organisation of the conference and the large number of speakers meant that sessions on different aspects
of the subject were held simultaneously in various small

meeting rooms. Melanie had gone carefully through the programme selecting papers which she felt would be of special interest to her and Bridget, for she planned to take notes and report back fully to her partner on each of the sessions she attended.

Obviously, the areas of patient care which concerned her were not those which interested her erstwhile medical colleague, for she did not see him in the sessions which she went to during the whole of the next day. She relaxed and enjoyed the stimulating discussion which followed each speaker, and felt she was being thoroughly enriched by the experience.

It was not until the very end of the day that she caught sight of Daniel Davenport, and it struck her how strangely alone and apart he seemed, even though he was speaking to a group of other people. As she approached the exit doors near which they were grouped, he saw her and disengaged himself.

'Ah, there you are!' he said pre-emptorily. 'Are you free to eat with me this evening?'

His breezy invitation hit Melanie unexpectedly hard. He was so infuriatingly cool! They happened to be here together in a foreign city for a couple of days, on professional business, and he was behaving as though she was available for 'off-duty' company in a way that he would never do back in London.

'Actually, I'm not,' she retorted with some satisfaction.

He had the grace to look somewhat taken aback.

'Ah!' he said.

'I have a previous arrangement for tonight.'

She left him standing there and walked out into the fresh air, where she gulped in a deep draught of it. I needn't have been quite so defensive, she told herself. I might not have been quite so offputting. Perhaps he genuinely wanted my company . . . oh, God! She thought back to how lonely and sad her impression of him had been only a few minutes ago . . .

'Melanie?'

Melanie turned to see who had called her name, half expecting the consultant to have followed her outside, but she could see him still standing where she had left him inside the glass doors of the conference centre.

A tall, slim elegant young man appeared at her side, wearing a quizzical expression across features which she barely recognised. Jan had grown into a very attractive young man, his sensitive face a male echo of his mother's.

'Jan!' she exclaimed. 'It's lovely to see you!' She had thrown her arms around him and was hugging him, suddenly overwhelmingly pleased to be with a member of her own family, however remote. He returned her warm greeting, his shyness evidently gone.

'I think you have forgotten your way to Scheveningen?' he grinned as they linked arms for the walk to the tram.

'I've even forgotten how to pronounce the name!' she laughed.

Her pleasure was only momentarily disturbed by the glimpse she caught of Daniel Davenport's cold stare as they moved away from the front of the conference hall. He can think what he likes, she thought defiantly, I'm tired of worrying about what he thinks of me.

It was good to talk to Jan over old family times and to find in him such a good companion. It was good to eat in the famous fish restaurant next to the sea. Afterwards, they walked together along the long, almost deserted promenade and had a cup of coffee in a bar frequented by Jan's student friends.

Back in her hotel room later, Melanie thought over the evening with pleasure, but decided, on reflection, that she did not envy her cousin his youth. She was glad her own muddled and rebellious student days were over and that she was firmly established in her chosen profession. She felt very sure that midwifery would fulfil all her professional ambitions. She thought of Ineke, who had combined career and family life so successfully. Then she thought about Ineke's young widowhood and how she had struggled singlehanded to bring up her son. Where would she have been without her work to fall back upon, both financially and emotionally?

It would be good to hear her aunt's paper tomorrow. Melanie felt a surge of anticipatory pride. Ineke had plenty to be proud of: her young son, and her professional achievement, thought Melanie, but most of all Melanie loved her aunt for her humility. It would be good to see her addressing a meeting of medical personnel and receiving their recognition as an expert in her own field.

Melanie was not disappointed. Ineke Aarts' contribution to the conference was heard by a huge audience and she gave a magnificent paper on the contribution of the midwife to reducing pain during childbirth without the aid of drugs. Melanie saw the tall figure of Daniel Davenport propping up the wall at the back of the room along with the many others who could not get seats at this, the last session of the meeting.

Afterwards, he beat her to her aunt's side downstairs in the entrance hall, and as Melanie approached, she heard him congratulating her on her talk.

'But it is rather unusual for you to deliver people at home in England, isn't it?' her aunt was returning sweetly.

'Not so unusual,' said Dr Davenport as Melanie joined them. 'Your niece is doing her best to reverse our policies of hospitalisation.'

He gave Melanie a slightly caustic look, which hardened as Jan materialised at her side once more. He had not told her he would be attending the last session, and he gave her surprised face a quick greeting kiss.

She had to control her splutter of laughter at the frank look of disapproval which this gesture received from the consultant, and at her aunt's amusement.

'This is my son, and Melanie's cousin, Jan,' she smiled. 'Dr . . . er . . . Davenport, wasn't it?'

'How do you do?' Daniel Davenport's demeanour seemed to relax visibly. He shook Jan cordially by the hand. 'Yes, your niece and I worked together up until quite recently at Lessing Lane,' he informed Ineke, 'until she went off in her own direction. I'm not quite sure what that is!'

Melanie controlled herself and smiled at him with some genuine warmth. It was the way he had described their having worked 'together'. One day, she was thinking, she would tell Ineke all about this legendary working relationship. But the next minute she was shaken out of her comfortable reverie by her aunt's words.

'Would you like to join us for dinner tonight?' she was asking the consultant. 'I am sure you would be most welcome, Dr Davenport.'

In an instant, Melanie understood what her aunt was thinking. Ineke would be delighted to encourage contact between her niece and this handsome British medical colleague. She would think Melanie would welcome the opportunity. She was so simple and innocent in these things. And Melanie had hardly had time to talk to her, let alone to explain what had been happening in her life . . .

'No, thank you so much. It's most kind of you, but I've been invited to join some Dutch medical colleagues for dinner.' He cast Melanie a meaningful, if slightly amused glance. 'A prior arrangement, you understand.'

'Of course, Dr Davenport. Perhaps we shall meet again,' Ineke rejoined warmly.

'I hope so!' he said, and, waving perfunctorily as he did when leaving the ward before speaking to Sister, he disappeared.

'What a charming man!' said Ineke. 'If we had obstetricians of such charm and looks here in Holland I might have remarried long ago.'

'Oh, no, Mother, you would never have done that,' said her son with a wink at Melanie. 'You value your freedom too much.'

'That's true,' admitted Ineke. 'And anyway, love was a once-in-a-lifetime thing for me.' She took Melanie's arm and led her towards the exit doors. 'And I think that in this you are like me, Mella,' she said.

Melanie was combing her hair the next morning, having packed. She was already slightly concerned about the journey back to Schiphol, and was thinking about her arrival here three days ago, when there was a tap on her door.

'What time is your flight?' Dr Davenport wanted to know. He looked at her comb and then at her hair as it lay over her shoulders, and she felt herself blushing.

'Not until four,' she said.

'Same as mine. What are you doing until then?'

'Nothing much . . .'

'Then we'll have a look at these famous bulbs of theirs at the Keukenhof gardens,' he said, without waiting for her reply.

He took her there with the same lack of ceremony with which he had conducted their previous journey, and when they got to the gardens he paid for both of them and took charge of the visit as though it was a ward round.

But his oddly offhand manner could not dispel the magic of the gardens for Melanie. The great old trees in the parkland lifted their heads to the spring sunshine, drinking in the warmth and unfurling brilliant new foliage. The last of the daffodils nodded next to the bright blue hyacinths, and all were in such profusion that they almost took the breath away.

In the glasshouses Melanie gasped at the exotic orchids, blossoming secretly in their tropical retreat. And then they came to the tulips: thousands of them, each perfect. The purple and scarlet, gold and green of the flowers dazzled her. Melanie bent to examine the blooms, each inlaid with the black and purple blaze at its centre, dusted with golden pollen.

'They're exquisite,' she whispered, almost unaware of her companion beside her. And forgetful of his usual lead and her customary place behind him on ward rounds, she wandered on and on, up and down the brilliant ribbons of colour that ran from one end of the long glasshouses to the other, smelling the musky scent of the flowers and delighting in them.

When at last he reminded her of the time, she made regretfully for the gates of the gardens, stopping frequently to look for one last time at the beds which smouldered with colour beneath the trees.

Just before their flight was called, Dr Davenport excused himself, returning a few minutes later with a large bouquet. Melanie's heart turned over at the sight of him, but she controlled herself when she saw the bland expression on his face, and did not overreact.

Taking the tulips, she thanked him demurely.

'You didn't have to do that,' she said quietly, gazing into the scarlet bowls in their paper sheath.

'Well, I shouldn't think they'll last till London,' he responded bluffly. 'Hurry up, or we won't get there ourselves.' And he headed her unceremoniously towards their departure gate.

Tulips from Amsterdam, thought Melanie, feeling stupidly happy.

CHAPTER FOUR

THE first of May—already! Melanie stared at the calendar in disbelief. It was a sunny Friday morning. In fact, it was so fresh and clear that she had decided to walk to the practice, having left her car there and rushed off to a complicated delivery with Bridget the evening before. May the first! No wonder the sun is shining, she thought. And then she remembered the Ball.

She slipped out of her coat and began setting up for the morning clinic. The May Ball was held at the SWCH on the first of May faithfully every year, except when it fell upon a Sunday. The Ball was the biggest date on the hospital social calendar, and Melanie could not imagine how she had forgotten it. She and Rachel had even discussed it a couple of weeks before, Rachel saying that she wouldn't be going because it would remind her too painfully of last year with John, and Melanie wishing she hadn't promised to go with Joe . . .

Joe! He must have forgotten all about it too. She hadn't heard a word from him since the night he had kissed her. She had forgiven him for that, and remembered their friendship with the same old pleasure as before, but she had privately decided against going out with him again. Perhaps he had come to the same conclusion and had decided to let the Ball date slip discreetly by. But it was most unlike him to forget completely about it.

Anyway, it would be impossible for him to forget. Melanie recalled the colourful posters which appeared each year upon the noticeboards and in the staff rooms at Lessing Lane and throughout the SWCH. Each year there was the same air of anticipation and excitement; the choosing and buying of new evening dresses and the speculation over partners for the Ball. And each year up until now, Melanie had been invited by one of the junior medical staff, usually the shyest and most diffident on the unit, and without fail she had enjoyed their company and the thrill of the evening.

She wanted to go tonight, and no amount of hard work would dispel the longing, she knew that. The phone rang and she expected Bridget to say that she had been called out yet again and would be late in for the ante-natal clinic, but it was not her.

'Hello? Melanie? Joe here.'

'Joe! How are you?'

'Fine. Listen, I forgot about the Ball; clean forgot! It's tonight. You must think I'm an oaf. Have you got another escort, or have you forgotten our date?'

'Neither. I was just thinking about it.' Melanie smiled to herself, both at the agitation in Joe's voice and at her own relief.

'Are you still on for it? I mean . . .' Joe hesitated, 'I've dug out the tickets, and as far as I'm concerned . . .'

Melanie really couldn't wait to put him out of his misery.

'Yes, Joe, I'd love to come with you. Where shall we meet?'

'At the South-West residency? Around seven-thirty? Or would you rather I picked you up? I was just thinking about avoiding driving . . .'

'That's fine. I'll see you at the SWCH. And Joe?' She waited for his quiet 'yes'. 'Thanks,' she said.

He whistled audibly down the phone, in an expression of his relief.

'Thank *you*, Melanie. See you tonight, then.'

Melanie hung up thoughtfully. She was pleased that she would be going to the Ball after all, but her pleasure was tinged with anxiety. Once more she cursed the apparent impossibility of lasting platonic friendship with someone of the opposite sex. And then she cursed the irony by which the platonic mode seemed to be able to refuse to convert itself in the opposite direction. Immediately, Daniel Davenport's enigmatic face appeared in her mind's eye, refusing banishment.

She was glad to hear Bridget's key in the front door, and set to pulling out the case notes for that morning's clinic: the last preparatory job before the clinic began. Glancing down the list, she lighted at once upon the name of Julia Young. She found the notes and flicked them open. Her client was thirty weeks pregnant already. Time seemed to be playing tricks on her today.

'Bridget?' she called through to where her partner was washing her hands next door. 'Did you know, Julia Young's thirty weeks already? I can hardly believe it!'

'Time flies when you're happy—and busy,' her partner rejoined.

'It's amazing, you know,' Melanie remarked later, as they snatched a cup of coffee between clients, 'but I can hardly remember what it was like to work in a hospital now.'

'And I can hardly remember what it was like to work without you!' Bridget replied warmly.

The two midwives worked so easily and effortlessly together these days that even their huge workload was fairly easily borne. When the clinic routine failed to work optimally they talked about it and changed it. When either needed a rest, or simply to talk something over, they each felt free to make their need known to the other. Melanie had made several suggestions for improvement of clinic practice from her recent hospital experience, and Bridget had adopted many of her ideas. In her turn, Melanie had grown in self-confidence and was now fully able to shoulder her full share of the workload.

The satisfaction that she found in this was hard to describe. She had tried to do so again and again. She had tried to tell Rachel of the simplicity of her role as a domicilliary midwife compared to the complexity of her experience in hospitals. She had spoken of the process of learning to guide a mother-to-be through the natural process of childbirth, encouraging and educating her.

She never ceased to be amazed at the richness of the experience as she now witnessed it. In hospital she had been a relatively passive bystander while doctors managed deliveries. She had watched drugs being administered and drips going up, scissors and stitches being used, and had wondered time and again how necessary it all was.

Of course, she knew that very often the painkilling Pethidine was wanted, that the induction was welcomed and the episiotomy unnoticed. But not always. Sometimes she had felt the natural process had been spoiled for the woman. It seemed such a shame to treat a healthy blooming pregnant woman as a sick patient and to manage her pregnancy and birth as though it were an illness.

She still respected the many women who felt safer in hospital for the birth of their babies. But she knew that each woman had her own unique way of coping with her labour and that confidence in themselves was the key to a happy, healthy delivery.

She was really sad when she paid her last call on her clients these days. Last week she had been to see Edna Dupont and found her calm and coping splendidly with her two children. In common with all the practice patients, breast feeding had been successfully established and the infant was thriving. How different from Melanie's experience at Lessing Lane! She had sat for an hour with Edna, drinking tea and discussing all her problems and pleasures, yet she had been lucky if she had seen a post-natal patient at the hospital whom she had delivered herself.

She looked up with a start at a tap at the consulting room door. It opened and her first client wafted into the room. Although twenty-six weeks pregnant, Amina Chowdhary retained the grace and dignity of a young girl in her silken sari.

'Hello, Amina. Come in!' Melanie's heart always lifted at the sight of her. 'How are you?'

'I am well.' Amina sat down.

'Are you still working?'

'Yes. We are very, very busy. I must help my husband or he cannot manage the shop.'

'He'll have to manage alone for a while after you have the baby,' Melanie responded. She thought her client looked so fragile, although she seemed so strong and unperturbed by hard work.

Amina smiled shyly.

'After I have the baby, yes. Then we will manage alone.'

Melanie felt the curve of the baby's back and then the little head. Amina lay quite still on the examination couch.

'He is moving a lot?' she queried.

'Oh, yes, he is moving all the time,' Amina confirmed.

Melanie turned up the volume on the electronic foetal heart monitor and placed the microphone over the baby's heart. A steady thumping sound filled the room, and she watched a smile spread slowly across the solemn features of the mother-to-be.

'He is very strong?' she whispered with pride in her voice.

'Yes,' Melanie replied with an answering smile, 'he is very strong.'

An hour or so later, she heard Julia's jovial tones bidding Bridget good morning. Julia seemed to carry with her her own special brand of energy and whatever the weather or the time of day she spread sunshine around her. As usual, she had the last appointment of the morning, and Melanie looked forward to seeing her in a leisurely fashion.

Julia sailed into the coffee room, as stately as Queen Cleopatra's barge. She removed her Jaeger silk head-square, slipped out of her coat and took a seat. Melanie remembered the first time that they had sat here together and the nervousness and uncertainty that she had felt then seemed like a bad dream. Julia Young and she had become such firm friends that she had to remind herself sometimes of the professional relationship between them.

'How are you today?' she asked now.

'Marvellous!' said Julia. 'I've never felt better.'

Looking at her, Melanie could believe that. She could never have looked better either. Her crowning mass of fair hair shone, her eyes were bright and her complexion clear and flawless. She looked ten years younger than Melanie knew she was, and she appeared to carry her extra weight with ease.

So Melanie was not too surprised to find Julia's blood pressure steady, her urinalysis normal and her weight increase of half a kilo quite acceptable.

'Everything seems fine,' she said. 'Just jump up on the couch and we'll feel the baby.'

Julia did as she was bidden and Melanie began to palpate her abdomen. Melanie's expert fingers moved carefully over the unborn baby. It was lying upside down. Her face betrayed none of her feelings as she checked again. She felt a head pushed firmly up beneath the maternal ribcage on the right-hand side. She did a quick mental check as she confirmed the position of the baby. It was definitely a breech.

And Julia was definitely thirty weeks pregnant. At least. That meant that the baby had only a bare two weeks in which to turn before it ran out of space in which to do so. Melanie swiftly decided not to worry Julia with the possibility that the lie would not correct itself. Instead, she turned on the monitor and let Julia hear her baby's heart.

'I'm so glad everything's going so well,' she said as she climbed down from the examination couch. 'You'll never believe it, but I think I'm beginning to convince Malcolm of the advantages of home confinement. He's been a hard nut to crack, but I think he's finally coming round to the idea.'

Melanie's heart sank involuntarily. She had a sudden vivid picture of Julia in the middle of a very difficult labour and of the Professor's legendary calm evaporat-

ing as his worst fears were confirmed before his very
eyes. It could not happen! Julia could not have a breech
baby! It *had* to turn before her next appointment.

'You must have been working hard on him,' Melanie
managed to smile. 'It's one thing to be convinced in
theory, another when your own wife and baby are
involved.'

Melanie swallowed hard and prayed as she stood
behind her client, helping her on with her coat. She
prayed as she had never prayed before.

After Julia had gone, she found Bridget writing up
notes and told her the news.

'She's got two weeks for it to turn,' she said.

'I hope it does,' returned Bridget. 'I really think it
would be too much of a risk to deliver a breech at home,
especially as it might be a long labour at her age.'

Melanie's face screwed up. 'I couldn't bear it if anything went wrong for her,' she said.

'I know how you feel,' Bridget replied, 'but don't get
into too much of a state over this. We'll just have to wait
and see what happens. Is she sure of her dates?'

'Pretty sure. You know what Julia's like. I'm pretty
certain that it's too big to turn already. And it had its
head down beautifully only last week.'

Melanie took a sip of scalding coffee and Bridget
sighed philosophically. 'That's how things go,' she said,
'but Nature works in strange ways . . .'

The shrill notes of the telephone interrupted them yet
again in the middle of their conversation. Melanie was
sure it would be Joe again, but when she picked up the
receiver it was Toby Robertson's smooth voice that
reached her ears.

'Ah, the lovely Melanie! How are you?'

'Very well, thanks,' Melanie responded coolly. She
caught Bridget's eye, mouthed Toby's name and almost
giggled at her partner's response. Bridget seemed much
amused by Melanie's attempts to keep the young GP at
arm's length.

'You've seen my patient Julia Young this morning, I

believe. How are things with her?'

It was incredible that Toby should choose today to ring and ask after Julia; he made no regular habit of doing so. Melanie swallowed hard and then took the plunge.

'Well, everything's fine, Toby, except that the baby's lying upside down.' She forced her voice to sound natural. 'I'm not worried about it really. It's sure to turn into a normal cephalic presentation by thirty-two weeks,' she added cheerfully.

'She's thirty weeks now, isn't she?'

'Yes, that's right.'

'Well, how about meeting me for a drink tonight to discuss the pros and cons of home confinement for breech presentations?' Toby suggested jauntily.

Melanie was speechless. Not only had Toby launched into her precise worst fear, but she felt his remark was in extremely poor professional taste.

'I can't do that,' she said eventually, 'because I'm going to the May Ball at the South-West City Hospital.'

There was a long pause at the other end of the line.

'I'm confident—or pretty sure anyway—that the baby will turn, Toby,' Melanie said desperately, trying to neutralise what had become an extremely uncomfortable phone call.

Bridget caught her eye, understood, frowned and placed her finger across her lips in a mimed warning to say no more. Melanie suddenly thought of a brilliant idea.

'Toby? Toby, if you fancy coming to the Ball, I know my flatmate needs a partner. She's very nice. I'm sure you two would get on really well. Would you like to ask her? I think she's on duty in the Special Care Baby Unit at Lessing Lane this afternoon . . .'

'A blind date, eh?'

Melanie could not read Toby's voice, but it had softened and she thought she heard mild interest.

'She's called Rachel,' she went on, 'Rachel Lewis.'

'But is she as delicious as you?' Toby teased.

Melanie didn't answer. She basked in her own relief.

'See you tonight, then, I hope,' said Toby. 'You'd better give me a dance.'

Melanie panicked the moment she had put the receiver down. She hoped Rachel would not mind. Melanie had detected a good deal of regret in her friend over the Ball. She knew that the end of her romance with John Edwards had been bad and that it had followed hard on the heels of last year's Ball. But Melanie had not liked the ambitious young consultant gynaecologist and had privately been pleased that Rachel was free of him. Still, there had been times over the past year when she had felt sorry for her feelings. Rachel had had one or two casual boy-friends since, but mostly she had been alone. And Rachel did not thrive on being alone, without a man around her.

Unlike her flatmate, thought Melanie wryly, who's used to it. She made herself think of Rachel and Toby Robertson. And the more she thought about them, the more certain she was that her idea might just have been a real inspiration.

'But what's he like, Mella, really? He's got a lovely voice on the telephone.' Rachel's blue eyes searched Melanie's dark ones for clues. 'You can't just go on saying "Wait and see" and "I'm sure you'll like him". It's not fair!'

Melanie smiled. Far from being upset at Melanie's intervention in her plans for this evening, Rachel seemed genuinely pleased and excited.

'He's quite presentable and a very good general practitioner. Nice to his patients . . .'

'Nice to his patients! A good GP!' exploded Rachel. 'What do I care what sort of GP he is?' She fell spluttering with laughter on to her bed.

Melanie surveyed her friend, then giggled too. It was nice to be going out together for a change, and nice to be back on close terms again at last. Melanie had not realised how much she had missed these crazy exchanges, typical since their student days.

Rachel sat up and attempted to bring some order to her blonde curls. She was already dressed for the Ball, in a stunning sheath of turquoise, the tiny shoulder straps of which accentuated her smooth white shoulders. Real drops of turquoise fell from her earlobes beneath the golden hair and gave an extra impression of slender height when she stood up.

'You look ravishing,' said Melanie.

Rachel ignored the compliment. 'Will he be nice to *me*? That's what *I* want to know.'

'I'd stake my life on it,' said Melanie. 'Zip me up, will you, Rach?'

Rachel did so. 'You're a dark horse, Mella. Fancy you keeping in touch with old Joe Peters! And I thought you two were just good friends at Lessing Lane.'

'We were. Are,' added Melanie quickly.

'Oh, that's fantastic!' Rachel breathed as Melanie turned round.

She wore red: the colour that she had adopted since the beginning of the year to match her new life and one which seemed to suit her so well. Her new Japanese silk dress fell straight to the floor from the high collar and cut-away shoulders, its crimson line alight with embroidered dragons and pagodas. The dress had seemed deceptively demure when Rachel had first seen it, lying on her flatmate's bed, but now that it clung to Melanie's hips, she saw its true allure. Melanie moved unselfconsciously into the middle of the room, her long dark hair free, stooping to see the skirt of her dress.

'Is this side slit too high?' she asked in a worried tone.

'Of course it's not. That's how Japanese ladies wear them. You're far too modest, Melanie.'

Recalling how Joe had lunged at her, Melanie tended to feel that modesty would be prudent. At least she felt comfortable in the dress, she thought, much more comfortable than she would in anything more revealing.

'All I can say is, if you're not in love with Joe Peters,

that dress is wasted on him,' said Rachel, turning
Melanie's thoughts into turmoil.

She made a pretext of combing her hair so that Rachel
would not see her blush. How she envied Rachel her
happy-go-lucky attitude! And yet she herself had never
bothered too much about her escorts before this evening. She had gone happily to the Ball prepared to enjoy
herself, and she had done so.

Why should it be different tonight? Yet she knew it
would be different. She knew she would not laugh so
readily, nor eat so enjoyably, nor dance so happily as she
had done other years. And she resisted and resented the
knowledge. She did not want to be stopped from enjoying herself by an absent phantom—and that was what
Daniel Davenport would be this evening. He would be a
ghost missing from his usual haunts.

She looked long and hard at herself in the full-length
mirror and forced herself to think about Dr Joe Peters.
But she could not budge the face from her mind: a face
overshadowed with past pain, yet smiling sardonically at
the present—at her!

'Are you ready?' asked Rachel. 'You've been doing
your hair for an age, and it's perfect. I'll get our coats.'

Melanie drove them carefully to the SWCH, trying to
dispel the ache that had begun inside her while she
dressed. She was disgusted with herself for allowing it to
overcome her this evening, of all evenings. Ever since
her return from Holland she had worked at banishing all
memories of Daniel Davenport, and she had prided
herself upon her considerable success.

She had almost never thought about the shiver of
pleasure and surprise which the touch of his hand had
generated in her on the plane. She had almost erased the
mental picture of his face as, unconscious of her stare, he
had cast about the reception hall for a familiar colleague
with whom to talk. She had tried to dissolve the spell
which he cast upon her inner life.

But the memories were never truly laid to rest. They
would rise up and she would find herself dreaming in

broad daylight, a set of notes idle in her hands. She had begun to take a longer route home to the flat from the practice so as to completely avoid the area of Lessing Lane. And the more she tried to ignore her inner disquiet, the more intense it grew.

Again and again she had gone over all she knew about him until the gossip and her own intuition became scrambled together, out of all recognition of the separate facts. But two remained intact: that Daniel Davenport was totally inaccessible to her as a man, and that as an obstetrician he harboured some strange mistrust of midwives—and of her in particular. It was strange, but painfully obvious to her that this last was so, but it was no easier for her to live with the former than the latter fact.

She backed the car into a space in the rapidly-filling staff car park behind the doctors' residency. Well, this was it! She was going to spend the evening with Joe and she would do her very best to enjoy it. She made a final effort, remembered that Dr Davenport did not attend hospital social functions, and at last managed to feel real relief that she would not have to bump into him with his wife—or whatever—and that was something to be thankful for.

'Melanie, come on! You're miles away. We'll miss the cocktails.'

Rachel leaned across and opened Melanie's door for her. 'You're in a funny mood tonight,' she smiled. 'I suppose Joe's a bit of an improvement on all those awful shy studious types who used to ask you to this do? About time too. I never understood why you agreed to come with them. Out of pity, I suppose.'

Rachel wasn't the only member of the staff at Lessing Lane who would be pleased to see Melanie with Joe Peters tonight. Plenty of the staff midwives had tried to forge a connection on more than professional grounds between the witty, radical Senior Registrar and his midwife counterpart. She had fended off many a pointed remark directed at her by colleagues whose sharp eyes for romance were matched only by their ability to spot an obstetric complication at twenty paces.

'He's nice, but we're really just friends,' Melanie reiterated. She drew her coat about her. They could see throngs of people gathered around the residency entrance. A small thrill of pleasure and anticipation tingled down Melanie's spine.

'I'll tell you tomorrow whether that's true or not,' Rachel returned, 'and I'll tell you whether your friend Toby Robertson is a good GP or not!'

Melanie gave her friend an old-fashioned look, then she pushed open the doors to the residency. A warm rush of perfumed air met her. A crowd of semi-familiar faces surged around her and she held tight to Rachel's arm in case they got separated. Everybody seemed to be talking at once, helping one another out of coats, admiring each other's appearance or greeting one another.

'The cloakroom's usually this side for us.' She managed to edge them both past groups until they reached the comparative peace of the queue at the cloakroom. There was another wait for space at a mirror for a final critical look at their faces before Melanie and Rachel finally emerged again into the now clearer entrance hall.

Melanie saw Joe straight away. He was tall, dark and, she had to admit, surprisingly handsome in evening dress. She waved and, with Rachel beside her, made for where he stood. His face told her at once how she appeared to him, and she read it with mixed feelings. Much to her relief, though, he did not publicly compliment her, but smiled at Rachel too and told them both that they looked great.

'You're not going to tell me I've got you both to myself?' he quipped. 'Melanie, I had no idea you'd bring Rachel Lewis as chaperon. What a bonus!'

'Cheek!' laughed Rachel. 'You don't know when you're lucky, Dr Peters, whether it's turning a breech or taking Melanie to a ball!'

Melanie shivered at the unwitting allusion to her great worry over Julia, and managed a smile at her flatmate.

'Oh, I know when I'm lucky all right,' asserted Joe, allowing himself a long look at Melanie.

She turned and searched the sea of faces for Toby Robertson's. He must arrive soon. Already the waitresses were circulating amongst the guests with trays laden with orange juice and Martini and sherries. The three moved through the crowds towards the huge double room which had been created for tonight by opening dividing doors between the big twin billiard rooms. Tables set with snowy linen fringed the room, and beyond a dance floor, a band could be heard assembling.

It was amazing the transformation in people that evening dress produced. Even the dullest, most matronly of the nursing officers was beautiful tonight. Everyone stood two inches taller than they usually did and looked with new interest at one another. Melanie felt her own heart lift in response to the familiar scene which was so strangely unfamiliar.

'Ah, here you are!' Toby grasped her elbow and turned her round to face him. For an instant she was confused—that face, those blue-grey eyes—but then she found her breath to greet him. She accepted his appraising look calmly.

'Toby—thank goodness! I wondered where on earth you were. Rachel?' She turned her friend around to meet the newcomer too, just as Joe arrived with three glasses of dry sherry. 'Rachel, this is Toby Robertson.'

She watched their eyes meet and knew that she had done the right thing in bringing them together for this evening. She introduced Joe to Toby, and watched him hail a waitress to bring another drink. How she would fare with him was another matter. Toby was gazing at Rachel and Rachel at Toby. Melanie decided firmly to get the evening off to a fresh start. 'A blind date,' she whispered to Joe. 'Where shall we sit, Joe?' she asked aloud. 'Let's find a nice intimate table for four where we can gossip unashamedly and really enjoy ourselves.'

'That's better,' said Joe with satisfaction. 'I was

beginning to wonder where my old friend Melanie was tonight.' He took her arm and led her to a corner table, indicating to the other couple to join them, but Toby and Rachel were talking, totally engrossed in one another already.

'Love at first sight,' remarked Joe laconically. He shook his head as if the very idea mystified him.

Melanie laughed.

'It does happen,' she said, as they took their places.

'Not to me it doesn't,' Joe replied. 'My relationships need long slow maturation, like fine wine or good cheese,' he explained, 'it's all a matter of taste.' He gave her a mischievous look.

'Is it?' asked Melanie innocently. The idea of Joe having been involved in a long relationship had not, for some reason, ever occurred to her.

'You're looking very lovely tonight, Melanie,' Joe said softly.

She recoiled. 'Thank you, Joe. You're looking pretty good yourself. Oh, look, here come the other two,' she added with relief.

Rachel was looking at Toby, who was guiding her expertly through the tables towards them. He was evidently totally at ease among the hospital staff, almost all of whom must be strangers to him. Something about his manner and his confidence struck at Melanie's secret heart. This was exactly how Daniel had been when he had first arrived at Lessing Lane: cool, calm, unperturbed by being an unknown quantity.

She tore her attention away from the young GP and gestured her flatmate to sit next to her. The tables all around were filling up with couples, the immaculate black and white of the men's evening dress providing a backdrop for the rich colour and movement of their partners' dresses.

They took turns to queue at the buffet for salads, and the men went back for more. Melanie ate pink shrimps and then rare roast beef, so tender that it melted in her mouth. She ate crisp lettuce and exotic salads of avocado

and oranges, and drank the cool white wine which was
brought to their table and replenished as the bottle
emptied.

It was only a matter of time before she warmed to the
talk and to the thrill of this occasion again. The subdued
hubbub of eaters at other tables, the clink of glasses and
the chink of cutlery became mere background to the
conversation that spread between the four of them.
Toby and Joe liked each other and vied for the girls'
attention with medical anecdotes of highly dubious
origin and content.

By the time they were drinking their coffee and
choosing chocolates from the little dish in the centre of
their table, Melanie was completely at her ease.

The band began by playing a gentle waltz to try to lure
the first dancers out on to the floor. There was an
answering rustle and stir as couples left their tables.
Waitresses moved in immediately, clearing plates and
leaving the tables clear but for wineglasses, candles and
miniature vases of single flowers.

Nothing was said between Rachel and Toby, as they
left their seats and moved towards the dance floor. For a
moment, Melanie watched them, hoping that Joe would
not ask her to dance just yet, but he caught her eye
determinedly.

'Come on, Melanie,' he prompted.

She followed him obediently through the sea of tables.

Daniel Davenport's hand froze halfway to his lips and
he lowered his glass gently to the table. Melanie had
stopped in her tracks as though she had seen a ghost, and
Joe walked on, unaware that she was no longer following
him. There were three tables between where she stood
and the quiet corner in which was set the consultant's
table for two.

While he watched her, and she stared at him, she
seemed to burn like a red flame in the centre of the
room. Seated opposite to him was a beautiful dark-
haired woman. She was dressed exquisitely simply in
sheer black. The candlelight glowed on her skin. She

watched the dancers taking the floor, quite unaware of Melanie.

Melanie came to herself, searched for Joe, and practically stumbled after him. He had waited for her at the edge of the now crowded floor.

'I thought I'd lost you,' he said with relief, taking her in his arms. Melanie danced mechanically. So he was here! She could hardly hear the music for the tumult inside her. And he was married after all. She had seen the bright golden band encircling the third finger of his lovely partner's hand; it had been quite unmistakable.

She felt Joe's arm tighten around her waist, and herself drawn closer towards him. Too numb to resist him, she allowed herself to yield to his embrace. His lips brushed her hair and then her face. She did nothing to stop him. She simply longed with all her being for the music to stop, and the moment it did so she pulled herself away from him and moved away.

'Wait for the next one, Melanie,' pleaded Joe.

What was the matter with her? The hurt in Joe's eyes accused her. She could not go on treating him like this for no good reason. She had to pull herself together. With a huge effort, she took his hand.

'I'm sorry, Joe,' she said softly, 'of course I will.'

She allowed herself to be drawn towards him once more and, fighting to relax, she tried to enjoy the dance. But when he kissed her bare arms and shoulder she drew violently away from him again. The dancers surged around them, oblivious of all but their own partner, and Melanie felt her arm brushed by the solid back of a man near her.

It was Dr Davenport. The next second, he turned his partner and looked over her smooth tanned shoulder into Melanie's face. His eyebrows lifted infinitesimally, then he lowered his head towards the woman until his own fair hair met her shining dark chignon. A stab of anguish shuddered through Melanie and she felt herself go rigid in Joe's arms.

'What's wrong, Melanie?' His lips caressed her earlobe. 'What's upsetting you this evening? You needn't be frightened of me. I shan't offend you again—I promise.'

'I'm not frightened of you, Joe,' she whispered, 'I'm just tired, I think, that's all. I'm sorry.'

'We'll sit the next one out,' he said, leading her off the dance floor before the music died again. She was so glad to pass the empty table for two before its occupants had taken their places again that she arrived back at their own table quite calm.

Joe was considerate and kind. He responded to Melanie's 'tiredness' with sensitivity and made himself extra amusing for her. He did not ask her to dance again. Now and then, Toby and Rachel joined them for a drink and a few minutes' talk, but mainly they danced, closer and closer as the evening wore on. It was almost midnight when Toby turned to Melanie.

'Hey, nearly the whole evening gone and you haven't given me that promised dance yet!' He was flushed with wine and excitement. Melanie had never seen him looking so relaxed. He was oddly attractive. 'Come on! No excuses, now,' he insisted.

Melanie rose from her seat, trying to avoid Joe's hurt look.

'She's lovely, Melanie!' Toby was warm and more genuine than Melanie had ever known him. 'I mean, you've done me a priceless favour.'

'I'm really glad, Toby.'

For the first time that evening, Melanie danced. She felt every beat of the music and the joy of her own natural response to it. Toby kept smiling at her as though he couldn't stop, and now that she knew what he was smiling about, she found herself joining him. When he asked her for a second dance, she happily agreed.

She had hoped for another fast number, the sort she loved to lose herself in, and was disappointed to see the lighting dim in anticipation of a slow dance. But when the song began she knew she could not leave the dance floor.

'Do you mind?'

Toby stopped just as he was about to put his arms around Melanie. He recognised the speaker as Daniel Davenport only with difficulty in the low light, and stood aside with a smile.

'My pleasure,' he replied, and gave Melanie a nod and a wink before disappearing in the direction of her flatmate.

Melanie felt light pressure about her waist as Dr Davenport led her to a less populated area of the dance floor, then took her gently but firmly into his arms.

She felt him fold her against her until she thought she would never breathe again. His hands found the naked skin of her shoulders, ran lightly over them, then down the satin sheen of her dress to her waist. She melted herself against him as though all her life had led her here.

'The first time ever I saw your face, your face, your face . . .' The lovely dark voice caressed them both, holding them together with its declaration, binding Melanie mutely to him with her own.

'I felt the earth move . . .'

His embrace tightened around her and Melanie felt faint. He said her name, almost inaudibly—or perhaps it was her imagination. Then he gently released her. She hardly dared to meet his eyes for fear of what she should find there, but when she did so, she saw such seriousness there that there was no doubt of his sincerity. He held her lightly for the remainder of the song, his former urgency gone, and as the last notes fell away, he let her go.

'You can go back to one of your many admirers now,' he said strangely, softly, 'Melanie.'

The warmth that his hands had left upon her dress beat through her body. She felt him move away with dismay, as if part of her went with him.

'Oh, no!' she heard herself breathe.

'What did you say?'

An endless moment passed before the band struck up

a noisy final farewell jig and people began to pour back on to the dance floor.

'Nothing . . .'

Melanie shook her head, shocked at the end of the perfect moment and at the people who surged round them. He strode ahead of her and Melanie, following, became aware again of the woman who sat alone, waiting for him. She forced herself to look at her. There was something about her face . . . she must have seen her around the hospital, perhaps, waiting for him to finish work . . .

'Thanks,' said Dr Davenport, almost dismissively, before he joined her again.

Melanie made her way back to her table, but her mind stayed with him. Soon afterwards the Ball formally ended, and Rachel insisted on Toby and Joe being asked back to the flat for coffee.

Melanie drove Joe, and Toby and Rachel went in his car. Melanie hardly heard what Joe was saying on the way back. The conversation over coffee was equally lost on her. She justed wanted to get to bed.

It was nearly three by the time the men left—if Toby left at all. Melanie accompanied Joe to the door and gave him as friendly a goodbye as she was capable of at that hour. She felt so sorry for him and for the way she had behaved that she submitted more readily to his kiss than she wanted to. Her feelings were in chaos and she was exhausted. It was Joe who drew away, as if afraid of his own passion. She wished him good night and went inside, leaving the door ajar for Rachel, who had gone for a walk with Toby.

In bed, Melanie half slept, half dreamed her endless dance with Daniel Davenport.

CHAPTER FIVE

JULIA YOUNG was not her usual self. Melanie, who had awoken more cheerful than she had since the morning of the Ball a fortnight before, sensed the reason straight away, and her heart sank in anticipation.

'Malcolm tells me that this little mite of ours is still a breech,' Julia said the minute she had come into the consulting room. Melanie had told her the truth the week before. Julia climbed unceremoniously up on to the examination couch. 'I'm not so sure,' she said. 'Tell me he's wrong, Melanie.'

Melanie palpated her abdomen with meticulous care. There, sure enough, was the little head exactly where it had been before beneath the maternal ribcage. Only now it was wedged there tighter than ever. Julia was watching Melanie's face.

'I'm sorry, Julia,' she said, 'but the Professor is right: the baby's still upside down.'

Julia looked heavenward. It was oddly disconcerting to find her so down. Melanie hardly knew how to comfort her. She watched Julia's features relax momentarily as she listened to the strong beat of the baby's heart, but then she relapsed into her preoccupation again. Melanie gently talcum-powdered her abdomen and, before Julia could know what was happening, attempted to turn the baby by external cephalic version.

Julia realised quite quickly, though, and her excitement tensed the muscles of her abdominal wall so that they tightened against Melanie's hands and thwarted her attempt to slide the baby around.

Julia got down from the couch with a sigh of disappointment.

'What shall we do?' asked Melanie, respectful as ever of Julia's right to direct her own care. 'We can try to turn it again next week ourselves, or leave things be, or get an ultra-sound done to check your dates, and possibly ask them to try to turn the baby at the hospital.'

Julia looked thoughtful. Melanie thanked fate that the waiting room was empty next door and that Bridget had settled down to paperwork in the office. If she had to go to Lessing Lane with Julia, at least she could get away from the practice without too much difficulty today.

'An ultra-sound, I think, if that's possible,' Julia said at length. 'Malcolm did mention it to me as a possibility —but of course I had to come to the decision myself. Bloody female pride, he calls it.'

'Quite a healthy commodity,' smiled Melanie in return. 'Sit down over here, Julia, and I'll ring Lessing Lane and try to arrange everything for today.'

She rang the familiar number and asked directly for Daniel Davenport. Because she was working, she seemed to have no trouble whatsoever in giving him the facts concerning Julia and asking for his help in confirming them.

'If you present yourself and your patient in a couple of hours, Miss Aarts,' he responded, 'I'll have arranged the ultra-sound, and I'll have a word with Mrs Young myself. If you don't mind.'

Melanie was pleased that the ultra-sound had been so easily and quickly arranged. The sooner they had Julia's dates confirmed the better, for then, if it was not too late, another attempt could be made to turn the baby.

This second drive to Lessing Lane with a patient for ultra-sound was very different from the first that she had made with Edna Dupont. It was late lunchtime and shoppers were hurrying back to their work in offices, leaving the streets to housewives with their prams. The trees were bright with new leaves and pink and white blossom hung in the many fruit trees like bridal lace.

Sitting next to Prof. Young's wife, Melanie felt a strange sense of protection towards her client. She knew how important it was for Julia to have her baby as naturally as possible and how brave she was being about this setback. On the other hand, Melanie would not let her take any risks. And if it was going to be dangerous to have her baby at home, she would have to work with Julia towards preparing her for a hospital delivery.

She glanced at Julia's profile and was struck by a likeness to another face which she had recently seen. But it was the appearance of Lessing Lane and the familiar buildings, she felt sure. It was so odd to turn up here with Julia Young—and in her new role too. She still had not got used to viewing the old place as anything but her own place of work.

Julia Young shivered. 'Thank God Malcolm's examining in North London today,' she said, 'so at least we'll be spared a public meeting here.'

'Poor Julia,' Melanie murmured. 'It is difficult for you.' She looked at Julia. 'And Dr Davenport said he wanted to see you too.'

'Oh, that's all right,' Julia replied more cheerfully, 'I can cope with *him*!'

Well, that's more than I can, thought Melanie, then put her private thoughts firmly behind her.

The ultra-sound technician was a fresh-complexioned blonde whose experience showed in the calm smooth way in which she worked. The routine procedure was carried out quickly and efficiently, although not so speedily as to cheat Julia of her opportunity of seeing her baby for the first time. She was thrilled at the shadowy picture, and for a moment, the joy of knowing certainly that the child was not only alive but well completely outweighed any anxiety which she and her midwife shared about the birth.

'Dr Davenport wants you to go straight up to his office when you're finished here,' the technician told Melanie while Julia was getting dressed. 'I'm to bring these up in a minute.'

Melanie had never before had occasion to see the interior of the new consultant's office. A secretary let her and Julia in, then returned to her typewriter in a small adjacent room.

'Hello, Sarah!' said Julia familiarly, poking her head around the door. Apparently Dr Davenport would be up at any moment.

'That's Sarah, the secretary that Malcolm shares with Daniel,' explained Julia in a stage whisper as soon as they were seated in the consultant's room. 'So much for cutbacks in the NHS!'

They both turned at the sound of voices in the door-way and Melanie was in time to see the ultra-sound technician blessed with one of Daniel Davenport's rare and wonderful smiles. He took the traces from her and thanked her as though she had just given him the Crown Jewels. So he keeps all his scowls for the midwives, Melanie thought with gall.

She looked carefully around the office. It was the workplace of a busy professional man, and carried no trace of any personal life. A litter of marked and open textbooks covered the desk. There were no family photographs such as those which stood upon the desks of other doctors in the hospital. Books filled the shelves to one side of the desk, and on the other side, he now closed the door discreetly between his room and that of his secretary.

'Mrs Young,' he observed, still smiling warmly, 'and Miss Aarts,' he added. 'Good afternoon.'

He shook them both engagingly by the hand. A professional relationship was firmly established. It was as if they had never met in any other circumstances.

For a moment or two he examined the ultra-sound pictures in silence, then he did some measurements of the baby's head.

'How many weeks, Daniel?' asked Julia, apparently unable to contain herself any longer.

He looked at her calmly. 'Thirty-one, Mrs Young.' He spoke with meticulous correctness. 'I wonder . . . Would you mind if I had a look at this baby of yours?'

Melanie had never seen such concern in his eyes.

Perhaps it was always there, and she had simply never seen him speaking to an anxious patient before. But anyway, she was amazed at his tact and his care with her.

'Well, I don't see why not,' said Julia bluffly, 'we've kept him to ourselves for a good long while, haven't we, Melanie?'

Melanie squeezed her hand briefly as he led them out of the office and into a private consulting room next door. It seemed really disorientating to be with him and a patient here, so far from the bustle of the everyday clinical areas.

She felt slightly unsure of protocol. He was treating Julia as though she were his private patient, and yet it was herself who was ultimately responsible for Julia's care. She decided to handle the situation carefully but firmly.

He turned his back while Julia climbed up on to the couch. He was washing his hands at the basin. It's as if he's two people, Melanie thought fleetingly. She stood close by while he palpated Julia and listened to the baby's heart. She watched his face change from that of the charming doctor to that of the alert, absorbed clinician. He powdered the abdomen and attempted external cephalic version.

Julia realised what he was doing, and Melanie watched the effort that she made to remain relaxed in order to help him. But it was not easy, especially for the second time in a few hours. Dr Davenport admitted defeat and abandoned his attempt with a resigned sigh.

'He's a determined little fellow!'

'Well,' said Julia, sitting up, 'it runs in the family, you know.'

He glanced at her, amusement in his eyes, as if a private joke had passed between them. 'You really do want to have this child at home, don't you?' he asked at last.

'Yes,' said Julia roundly, 'I do.'

Melanie looked at the obstetrician, meeting mutely but unmistakably his resistance to the idea. She sensed his anger and impotence. He was powerless in this situation, and he was not used to being powerless. His feeling was all concentrated into the look he gave Melanie.

'And how do you feel about that? *Now?*' he asked pointedly.

'We shall have to see,' Melanie demurred, 'sir,' she added. It was an automatic response. She did not mean to be servile, but being back here in the hospital she seemed to slip back into her old habits of behaviour towards him.

He gave her a glance of cold amusement, as if he read her thoughts.

'I should like to try to turn the baby again—next week, or sooner. If you feel able to let me try, Mrs Young?' He turned back to Melanie, questioning her without words.

She knew that she welcomed his help and expert opinion, and yet he insisted upon making her his enemy. He was so ill at ease that Melanie found herself lost for words.

'. . . but you'll want to have a private word together,' he said at last. 'Perhaps you'll meet me downstairs . . .' he glanced at his wristwatch. 'I must make a quick visit to the ante-natal clinic to see another patient. Could you stop by there on your way out of the hospital?' He looked from one to the other. 'You can talk here in my office, if it suits you.'

Melanie and Julia decided against testing the secretary's discretion too far, and found a far corner of the patients' waiting area in the ante-natal clinic for their discussion.

They sipped cups of good strong WRVS tea and Melanie thought, not for the first time, that these women volunteers should be paid more than consultants. She watched the volunteer lady listening kindly and sympathetically to a pregnant child of not more than eight-

een years old. It was a pity that she had not had such a
listening ear or sound mature advice sooner, Melanie
thought.

'Hello, Melanie!'

Joe, abstracted as always in Ante-natal, his white coat
half open and a sphygmomanometer in his hands, recognised her first and then, with a start, the Professor's
wife. His eyes questioned Melanie for an instant as soon
as he took in Mrs Young's physical condition. And then,
discretion itself, he excused himself. 'Forgive me, Mrs
Young, Melanie. Terribly busy this afternoon. Must
dash!'

As he passed behind Melanie he told her he would
pick her up that evening. She had no time to answer him.
Daniel Davenport appeared at the same moment.
Whether he overheard Joe's parting promise or not she
could not tell, but the consultant gave her a look of
withering disapproval.

For a moment she felt like a first-year student nurse
caught by Sister dating a patient on her first ward. And
then her innate self-respect reasserted itself. How dared
he make her feel like that? She had nothing to be
ashamed of. At that moment she decided that she would
enjoy Joe's company tonight, even if only to defy Daniel
Davenport.

'We've decided that we'd like you to try again,
Daniel,' Julia said positively, 'and then Melanie thinks
we can go forward from there.'

'She does, does she?' He threw Melanie an unread-
able look. 'Can you come back this time next week,
then, Mrs Young?'

'Yes. At least, *I* can. Will that be all right with you,
Melanie?' asked Julia.

Melanie nodded.

'I'd like a private word with you, if I may,' the
consultant told Melanie. He drew her aside, smiling at
Julia. The minute they were out of earshot, though, his
manner changed.

'If you get Mrs Young here for two next week, you can

come in an hour earlier yourself and have some lunch with me,' he demanded. 'I want to speak to you.'

'I'll try to manage that,' said Melanie, shaken, but dignified.

He marched off back to where Julia stood, without waiting for her to say more. She watched while he bade the Professor's wife a warm farewell. Jekyll and Hyde, she thought.

She rejoined Julia herself.

'Let's get out of here,' said Julia. 'We've been here long enough.'

Melanie could not have agreed more.

Outside in the spring sunshine Julia turned to her with her old cheerful smile.

'I feel like spoiling myself,' she announced, 'What shall we do?' She stopped. 'Oh, how selfish I am! You have to get back to the practice, I suppose.'

'No,' said Melanie with pleasure, 'I told Bridget we might not get back this afternoon, so she isn't expecting me. And I'm not on call. So what shall we do?'

Julia was delighted. 'We could have some posh tea at that place opposite Kew Gardens,' she suggested. 'Not that there's anything wrong with the WRVS variety, of course . . .'

Melanie laughed. She had passed the quaint old teashop at Kew many times on her way to and fro from Richmond, but she had never actually joined the elegant tea-drinkers there.

She drove slowly to Kew Green and parked on the edge of it, then together, she and Julia walked around the well-kept grass, admiring the fresh beauty of the chestnut trees that lined it.

The Regency houses and cottages looked truly regal in the year's first sun. Each seemed newly-painted and pristine.

'Aren't they lovely?' said Julia. 'We almost bought one when we got married, but they were a bit outside our price range. We thought we'd be poor for the foreseeable future—well, poor-ish, what with children coming along straight away . . .' She stopped short. 'You just can't tell how things are going to turn out, can you, Melanie?' she said. 'I mean, life is so strange sometimes. Of course, you can't have all these sort of worries, still so young and free . . .'

'Not so young!' laughed Melanie, 'but free . . . well, yes,' she paused and took in Julia's curious look. 'That's what they call midwives who practise independently in Holland,' she explained, ' "free" midwives.'

Julia gave her an amused sidelong glance. 'Well, well evaded, "free" midwife Melanie!'

Together they explored the antique shops which had sprung up like spring flowers around the Green. Their windows were full of irresisitible old things, from blue and white Willow Pattern plates to silver thimbles. Both women were entranced.

'Oh, look at that!' Julia pointed into a jumble of articles behind a dusty windowpane.

Melanie's eyes came to rest upon an old teething ring of mother-of-pearl. A tiny seated teddy bear of silver, a bell on each foot, was fixed to the ring.

'A Victorian teething ring!' exclaimed Julia ecstatically, 'exactly like the one I had myself when I was a baby. Oh, Melanie, do you think it would mean bad luck if I bought it? I really don't think I can resist it.'

Melanie hardly had time to reassure her. Julia disappeared into the shop, emerging a minute or two later with a tiny tissue-paper parcel. She unwrapped it and held the contents out for Melanie to see.

The little silver bear seemed to smile at her and the mother-of-pearl caught the sunshine and turned it into milky rainbows. The ring seemed to touch a chord inside Melanie. She could no more have touched it than caught a rainbow. She could hardly bear to look at it, it was so beautiful to her.

'How about a pot of tea and some cakes?' she heard herself say. 'I'm starving!'

'Oh, I am sorry, Melanie. I don't know what I'm

thinking about today. Completely wrapped up in myself,' said Julia.

When they had found a table in the teashop Julia spoke again. 'What sort of cake are you going to have?' she asked. 'It's my treat.'

'No,' Melanie replied, 'it's mine!'

'I'm going to have Maid of Honour,' said Julia with a secret smile. 'That's what they call bridesmaids in America: maids of honour.'

'Is it?' asked Melanie politely. She could not imagine why Julia should so have parodied her previous remark. She was still wondering about it when Julia next spoke.

'I don't want to have to go into hospital,' she said, her voice deadly serious now. 'It's not that I'm worried about hospital as such. Lessing Lane's lovely and nobody could be more attached to the old place than I am. It's more personal than that . . .'

Melanie waited quietly for her to continue.

'It's that . . .' Julia gazed into her teacup with a frown, 'Malcolm and I . . . I mean, it's been so hard all these years; the infertility tests and the worry. It's just so important to me that this is a private event, just between us and our closest people, in our own home. But it's so difficult with Malcolm. You see, he's so used to the public eye nowadays, and he won't think about it, but just be sad that it wasn't as it should have been . . . when it's all over and too late to make it right . . .'

'Yes,' said Melanie softly, 'I can see what you mean, Julia.'

'You really do, don't you?' said Julia, looking up into her eyes. 'Thank you for that, Melanie.' She lifted her cup and the mood of confidence was gone. 'Here's to our home delivery, then,' she said.

'Here's to it,' Melanie agreed.

It's in the lap of the gods, she was thinking. If the baby could not be turned by external cephalic version in the consulting-room next week, she would have to consider trying to turn it under the complete relaxation of a general anaesthetic. Daniel Davenport would be sure to suggest that next. And if all attempts to turn it failed and the breech presentation persisted, she would have to discuss the whole question of the delivery with Julia and her husband anew.

It was in the lap of the gods—and Daniel Davenport. If he could turn the baby next week, Julia could have her precious home delivery and everyone would be happy. Everyone? Melanie thought of the consultant. She reconsidered. Well, perhaps not quite everyone, she thought.

'It's Joe Peters!'

Rachel stepped back from the window in the living room and gave Melanie an old-fashioned look. 'You didn't tell me you two were still seeing one another.'

Rachel had a terrible habit of spying upon all who stopped their car within three doors of the flat, and of inventing their histories and purpose if she was not already in possession of it.

'We're not—not really. Not regularly,' said Melanie. But she felt herself blush out of sheer habit during Rachel's inquisitions of this sort.

'Toby's picking me up at nine. How nice that we're both going out. We can compare notes on the evening later. Have a lovely time . . .' Rachel called, as Melanie went to answer the door.

Rachel and Toby had been going out ever since the Ball, and their dates had become very frequent. Rachel seemed to go out every one of her free evenings. Melanie was really pleased for them both, not least because her working relationship with Toby had become so much more pleasant since he had met Rachel. And it was always lovely to be around Rachel when she was in love. It suited her, Melanie mused wistfully as she opened the door to Joe.

Joe eyed her neat, jean-clad figure with approval.

'I thought we'd walk somewhere,' he said. 'Maybe to the river?'

Walking, she realised what emotional tension she had

been under all day. It was heaven just to stroll along, with no particular thing in her head. She glanced at Joe. How odd it was with him, she thought. Today, in front of Julia Young, he had hidden his surprise at her pregnancy so completely, yet now she could read his face like a book. Why did he feel like this about her? She could not imagine how she had encouraged him to fall in love with her.

'I want to have a quiet talk with you, Melanie, preferably somewhere private. Is that all right with you?'

Melanie swallowed. 'Yes. I mean, of course. Why not?'

She had to fight a sudden and stupid blind desire to run all the way back to the flat and lock herself in her bedroom, just as she had done as a child.

'I've missed you since the Ball, Mella. I think we should see more of one another.'

She looked again at Joe and saw how serious he was. A stab of pity went through her. She couldn't let him continue like this. She had to tell him honestly that she would never be able to return his feelings. But she did not have time to find the words.

They had reached the river near where Melanie had been that afternoon with Julia. They walked down to where the trees threw shadows across the path in the early evening light. Joe caught her swiftly in his arms before she could protest, and pressed his mouth to hers.

She tried to return his kiss out of pity, knowing that it would be their last, but as his insistence grew she felt her whole self pulling away from him. She gasped his name.

He stared at her, as if stupefied by her refusal of him. She made out on his face an expression she had never seen there before, and for the first time, she mistrusted him.

'Let's go and have a drink, shall we?' she said, turning and regaining the path that they had left. 'There's a nice pub near here, if I remember.'

Joe did not answer. He walked stiffly and silently

beside her until, to Melanie's immeasurable relief, they entered the busy bar. Here, surrounded by noise and laughter, she felt blessedly safe again.

'I'll get the drinks,' she said. She struggled to the bar and ordered beer for Joe, and a Scotch for herself. If ever she had needed a drink, it was at this moment. Yet Joe was harmless enough. What had come over him? It was all that she could do not to swallow the whisky at the bar.

She made her way back to him, swearing to herself that there would be no more outings for them after tonight.

'Thanks,' he said, taking his drink, but avoiding her eyes.

She sat down opposite him and lifted her glass. But he had not waited for her to begin his own drink. The whisky left a hot trail down Melanie's throat to her stomach and took her breath away.

'So I shocked you into drinking Scotch, did I?' enquired Joe painfully.

Melanie thought it best not to answer. She tried to change the subject; to try to retrieve something sane from the encounter.

'You looked busy today. Is Ante-natal as hectic as ever? I thought they were going to change the appointments system to get rid of block booking?' There was no reply. 'I thought the spring rush was as good as over,' Melanie persisted.

'Well, I expect the more select patients wait politely until it is, so that they get everybody's full attention,' he said nastily.

Melanie stared uncomprehendingly at him for an instant. 'What do you mean?' she asked.

'I don't expect the wives of professors of obstetrics and gynaecology go in much for waiting in busy ante-natal clinics,' he replied.

'That's most unfair!' Melanie exploded, lowering her voice furiously. 'And if you're referring to my client, no such base consideration would ever enter her head.

She's not the snob you'd have to be to even think of such a thing.'

'What's she doing with you, then?' Joe asked flippantly.

Melanie could hardly believe her own ears, or her eyes, which told her of characteristics hitherto un-imagined in Joe Peters. Where was her loyal friend and professional champion now? Yet she could not bring herself to believe that such real friendship had been so shallow as to be dispelled by an unwanted kiss. She composed herself.

'She wants to have her baby quietly, in her own home, surrounded by her close family,' she stated quietly.

There was another uncomfortable silence during which Joe drained his glass.

'I think you're making a big mistake,' he said. 'I'm not going to ask you about your patient. Obviously. Natural delicacy as well as professional considerations prevent me from doing so.' He smiled ambiguously. 'But you wouldn't have been with her at Lessing Lane today unless there were complications. And complications are dangerous. Even in an eight-foot eighteen-year-old prima gravida . . .'

Melanie patiently took in the old joke, and then the very unambiguous message behind it. Joe was telling her that he thought Julia Young too old and too high-risk a case for her care.

'Thank you, Joe, for your professional opinion. Especially given the discreet surroundings.' She cast a furious glance around the occupants of the pub, any one of whom might be related to Julia and Malcolm Young in some way. Then she got to her feet. 'I'll walk home by myself, if you don't mind,' she said.

'Please yourself,' said Joe, remaining seated. 'You know what I think.'

Melanie made for the door. Outside she began to walk fast. And so that leaves Toby, she thought incoherently: the only remaining member of the medical profession to respect my professional capability. She could not believe she had lost Joe. She could not believe that she had sat not so long ago in a crowded conference hall full of doctors listening deferentially to her aunt as she described domiciliary midwifery.

She could not put the river and Joe behind her fast enough. But the fleeting thought of the conference had worked its magic. By the time she got back to the flat, tired and breathless, the memory of Joe's kiss had vanished behind older, sweeter and more disturbing recollections.

CHAPTER SIX

Two days later, Joe rang Melanie at the practice again.

'Hello,' he said. 'Melanie, what can I say? I'm very sorry. I was a pig.' His tone was light.

'That's all right, Joe,' she heard herself reply. She had not expected a placatory call from him, or these contrite words, especially not so soon.

'Melanie, I want to make amends. Can I see you?'

She had decided that she would not see him again, at least not for some time. It was obvious that she could not meet him outside the hospital without him feeling encouraged. And she could do without a friend who had proved himself so fickle. Remembering that evening strengthened her resolve.

'No, Joe. I think it's best if we don't see each other for a while. It was all a bit—um—unfortunate, wasn't it?'

'That won't happen again, Mella.' His use of her pet name, which he had picked up from Rachel at the Ball, irritated her. 'I was stupid. I can't think what came over me.'

'No, Joe,' she repeated firmly. 'Let's leave things as they are for a time. You know how I've always valued your friendship.'

'Until now . . .' His voice tailed off. He sounded wretched.

Melanie said goodbye as gently as she could, and hung up.

As she returned to her patient, though, Melanie's irritation with Joe reasserted itself. He had called her away from Amina at a crucial moment in their consultation. It was very rare for Amina to ask Melanie for special advice. Normally, she presented herself for her clinic visits in the same way in which she left after them: calmly and quietly.

110

But today had been different. After her routine tests and examination, Amina had hovered shyly in the doorway and Melanie had asked her to sit down again, sensing her disquiet. At last, Amina had admitted that her mother-in-law, who had arrived from the Punjab ostensibly to help her, was the cause of her worry.

Now she continued to explain in short, soft bursts of speech that told her of her anxiety.

'It is a very big difficulty to tell to her how life in England is different from life at home in India. She tells me that the ante-natal classes for natural childbirth are not necessary, that it is nothing to have this child . . . She has had six children,' she added meekly.

'And you've tried to explain that in this society we do things differently?'

'Yes. I thought, yes, my mother-in-law, the mother of my husband, she will be so happy that I do not have a male doctor. Just as my husband was happy. But she is not happy. She is angry that I go to these classes and that Ashad came with me and saw the film of a baby being born. It is not right, she says. It is a woman's business. And now my husband listens to her, because she is his mother . . .'

Amina was sobbing.

'It's very difficult for you,' Melanie soothed softly. She held Amina's shaking shoulder gently until the sobbing ceased. 'You must feel torn between your old life and your new. You've worked so hard since you came to live here. And you've been brave and strong.'

'Perhaps,' said Amina carefully, 'perhaps it will be very painful, and I will not be brave, and my mother-in-law will be even more disappointed in me.' Her large brown eyes, still full of tears, met Melanie's with pride and defiance. 'I do not want that,' she said.

'Amina, your classes are very important. The more you understand about the birth of your baby, the easier the birth will be. Both you and Ashad understand that. You've always wanted to share the experience—you've both told me so.'

Melanie lifted one of the delivery kits towards them and opened it on the table in front of Amina.

'Look, here are the things which I shall bring with me when the baby comes. Here are the tablets of tranquillisers and sedatives which I may offer you if you need them. Here,' she tapped the little glass phials of Pethidine, 'are the drugs that will stop your pain, if you need them.' She took out the standard inhalation equipment for use during labour and showed Amina the small cylinder of nitrous oxide. 'This is the Entonox about which you've learned in your classes. If you need it, it will be there for you.'

Amina's eyes were now clear.

'You will not disgrace yourself in front of your mother-in-law, Amina. Nobody can now know how your birth will go, but perhaps you'll be pleased that we've talked like this today, or perhaps you'll find that you won't need anything that I've shown you. But most of all, you must not be frightened. You've been so calm up until now. Your husband's mother will come to understand how differently you and your husband live now, I'm sure.'

'I hope it,' Amina responded softly.

'Are you still working hard, Amina, in the shop?'

'Not so hard. Soon she will begin to work in the shop, when she knows a little English. Now she does all my cooking.'

'That's good, Amina. You need to rest more. You're getting tired, and that's undermining your confidence.'

A few minutes later, Melanie closed the door gently behind her client, hoping she had managed to reassure her. Bridget came in as she was clearing up.

'Had a delivery?' she smiled, nodding towards the open equipment.

'Not quite,' Melanie returned. 'It was poor Amina. I was trying to put her mind at rest and show her that nothing could stop us from helping her during the birth if she needed pain relief. Her mother-in-law's frightened her half to death with her stories of how she's had six children without a pang or a complaining word. Honestly, I don't know which is worse: the woman who tells horror stories about her labours or the one who makes everyone else feel as though they're a weak freak. Women! Sometimes I wonder whose side they're on!'

'I know. Amazing, isn't it? Hours of careful ante-natal preparation dashed to the ground with a single careless word from someone close to home who should know better. The closer they are, the sillier it makes them sometimes.'

Melanie sighed. 'Anyway, how was Mrs Bush?'

'Fine! A beautiful healthy boy. Dad's delighted, of course, especially after the three girls. We had a deep transverse arrest, but I managed to turn his head, and then it was only another hour. She was very quick once we'd corrected the arrest.'

Bridget yawned, checked her bleep, then grabbed Melanie by the arm.

'Let's get out of here,' she grinned, 'before that blessed machine rings again!'

But in fact the practice had been much quieter lately. In spite of their twenty-four-hour on-call service, Melanie and Bridget had both been able to take regular days off, and they felt the benefit of them. They had both attended study days at the Royal College of Midwives and Bridget was due to attend her compulsory refresher course next month.

These brief courses organised by the College were a brilliant, uniquely British innovation which ensured that midwives stayed up to date and that their clinical practice did not rust for lack of new input. The courses were, Melanie knew, even envied in Holland where the well-developed midwifery service lacked any such self-regulating machine for professional improvement.

And Melanie was due to take a holiday. She and Rachel had been planning where they would go and what they would do, and after much debate, had decided on their usual plan—to go to

Rachel's sister in Brighton.

'Anyway, it's just as well we're going on holiday together,' said Rachel, over a rare shared supper one evening, 'we'll need a week to catch up on one another's lives.'

'And whose fault is that?' asked Melanie, helping herself to more carry-out curry. 'You're never in these days. How's the new love?'

'Lovely,' said Rachel dreamily.

'So's this tandoori chicken,' replied Melanie.

'No, really, Melanie—he's very nice indeed,' her flatmate answered, with emphasis on the last word.

Melanie looked up. 'What does that mean?' Something about the way Rachel didn't talk about Toby had raised her suspicions about their affair. She was sure it was much more serious than others had been.

'Nothing. Nothing!' Rachel's wide blue eyes radiated innocence. 'How's Joe?'

'I wouldn't know,' stated Melanie, with satisfaction.

'Oh?'

'I haven't seen him since you did, and I don't expect to do so—outside our apparently inevitable encounters in the ante-natal clinic at Lessing Lane,' Melanie added drily.

'Well, you're getting very superior about ante-natal clinic encounters. That's the way we lower mortals meet our men—if we ever do, that is,' said Rachel with exaggerated pathos.

'That's not how you met yours,' said Melanie, unmoved.

'Ah! Not *this* one. But then *this* one's different from all who have gone before . . .'

'I knew it!'

She said she was glad for them, and she was. She had nursed Rachel through too many broken love affairs not to be glad that they were a thing of the past. But she could not help feeling left out, feeling a nagging doubt about her own life. She thought about Joe. It was true, she did not find him particularly attractive as a man, but he had a nice sense of humour and he had been a good friend to her.

Perhaps she had been hasty in giving him the complete brush-off. For the first time, she realised how much she missed his sympathy. Perhaps she'd been hard on him.

'Perhaps there's something wrong with me,' she heard herself murmur, almost to herself.

'What's that, Mella?' asked Rachel cheerfully, finishing off the rice from the bottom of an aluminium container. 'You're mumbling.'

'I was just wondering if there was something the matter with me,' she repeated.

'The matter?'

'Well, you know. I don't seem to be very good at getting boy-friends.' It seemed ironical that now, the first time that she had ever spoken about her deepest fear to anyone, it should be addressed to Rachel. And yet there was nobody else whom she would tell. She hoped that Rachel would respect her and not tease her out of the mood that had descended upon her.

'Sometimes I'm surprised at you, Melanie.'

Rachel surveyed her friend shrewdly, even severely, and Melanie bore her scrutiny in painful silence.

'You expect one thing of yourself one minute and another the next. Why should you set your sights any lower personally than professionally? You were never satisfied until you got yourself out into private practice where you could be the sort of midwife that you wanted to be. It didn't matter how difficult it was for you or how difficult other people made it for you. Now why on earth should you satisfy yourself with Mr Average when it comes to choosing a man?'

Melanie laughed out loud. 'Well, I suppose . . . if you put it like that . . .'

'Of course I put it like that,' Rachel retorted. 'That's how it is! And if you've given Dr Joe Peters the push, it's because he isn't good enough for you and that's all there is to it. And one day someone will come along who is good enough . . .'

She stood up and cleared away the debris from the table in record time; foil dishes and paper into the waste bin and the rest thrown into the sink. She turned the hot tap on momentarily as a token to the washing up . . . 'and that will be that!' she added with a flourish of the wet cloth over the draining board. 'And now I must fly. Toby's furious whenever I'm late—which is always. The main feature will have started as usual.'

'Have a lovely time,' Melanie shouted after her. 'And don't forget to have a good cry at the end!'

It was Rachel's speciality to cry over films, books, television soap opera—anything with which she could remotely identify. Melanie never did. It was a well-worn joke between them. She thought about it while she did the washing up and then made herself a cup of instant coffee.

She took her cup over to the bay window in the living room and pulled a chair round so that she could sit and look out. She stared down through the still scantily-clad branches of the great walnut tree to the street below. Rachel's words still rang in her ears. There was no doubt that Rachel had put her finger exactly on Melanie's 'problem'. Mr Average, she thought ruefully; she's right, he's not for me. But what if I am not for Mr Right?

In her mind's eye, Dr Davenport smiled his most beguiling smile: the one he had bestowed on the air stewardess, the ultra-sound technician. And then he smiled a more intimate smile—the one that he had given Julia Young. That was much nearer to the expression he would use to a woman for whom he really cared.

She remembered his summons to meet him before Julia's next appointment. What did he want to talk to her about? The question, once resurrected, refused to lie down again.

With a sick sensation, Melanie put her half-finished coffee down on the floor beside her. She might as well brace herself for it. The appointment was only two days away. She was to be given another lecture—she was sure of it—on the risks of home confinement. But this lecture would shake her confidence far more than Joe's jibes had done. And this lecturer would have a trump card up his sleeve and would not be afraid to use it against her, fool that he thought her.

She didn't understand why he did it. She knew that instead of making her angry, as Joe had done, he would render her dumb with misery. And she knew that now that she had remembered it, she would live the meeting to come a thousand times before it actually arrived.

She did. She also worked as hard as she could at the rather quiet practice, and remembered to call Toby Robertson to tell him what was happening with his patient.

'I'd like to speak to Dr Robertson, please.'

'That's not possible at the moment—he's very busy. Can I take a message?'

These general practice receptionists, Melanie reflected impatiently, are more efficient than a personal bodyguard!

'No,' she replied politely, 'I'd like a word with him personally, but it's a professional call.'

'I don't mind what sort of call it is, dear, he's busy with a patient. I'll tell him who called. What's your name?'

'Melanie Aarts,' fumed Melanie.

'Fine. I've got that, dear. Goodbye for now.'

Melanie stood there with the dead receiver in her hands, then slowly hung it up. It began ringing immediately.

'Hello? Melanie? I am sorry. Mrs Baines is an angel, but a trifle over-enthusiastic in protecting me sometimes. What can I do for you?'

'Oh, Toby. I wanted you to know that I was taking Mrs Young up to Lessing Lane today for a second attempt at external cephalic version. Did you get my note about the first one?'

'Yes—thanks a lot, Melanie. I hope today goes better for you both.'

'You don't sound too worried. I'm so afraid it might

have to be a hospital delivery after all.'

'I'm not worried, Melanie. If it was left up to me, I'd leave you to deliver her at home, breech or no breech. You're an excellent midwife and she couldn't be in safer hands.'

'Thanks, Toby. But it could be a long labour . . .'

'And it could not. Plenty of bottom-first babies have been safely delivered at home. I was one myself. Oh, there goes one of my deepest secrets . . . You know the other one!'

Melanie giggled at this allusion to Rachel.

She was still smiling when she got into her car. She drove slowly up towards her old training hospital and every landmark seemed to have an amplified effect on her overstretched nerves. Toby's vote of confidence in her faded by the second.

The bulky masses that constituted the SWCH seemed even bigger than usual and the activity in the wards through the plate glass windows seemed even more certainly to exclude her. She could see the rails that carried the bed-screens, vases of flowers along the window-sills and the flitting butterflies of the nurses' white caps.

How long ago it all seemed: the first bed-bath—her first patient! She could remember his face, though, as if it were yesterday that Sister Tutor had prepared her for his care. 'Close the window, pull the screens, and tell the patient what you're going to do!'

Other early commandments crowded into her head. They amounted to a set of golden rules on which she had built her whole career, first in nursing and then in midwifery.

She turned into Lessing Lane and glanced affectionately out of her nearside window at the park, struggling valiantly to turn green. Through the grimy windows of her beloved maternity hospital she could see the midwives busy in the wards. She put her mental finger on the fulcrum of her change of career: the nurse cared for the sick, the midwife for the well woman.

She parked neatly, took a deep breath of fresh air,

then walked into Lessing Lane. She nodded a hello to the porter on duty—a new man whom she did not recognise—and got into the creaking lift. Two new young pupil midwives in their pretty dark pink dresses and white caps joined her. They were in the middle of an excited discussion.

'. . . then he said, "Pupil Midwife Barnes, there's quite a considerable difference between an average orange and a Jaffa orange. I said that the uterus at eight weeks will be the size of the former, at ten weeks the latter." The patient was giggling so much I could hardly palpate her, then she said she'd have to go to the loo. "Umm. Displacement of the uterus by a full bladder —very tricky."' The girl puffed out her chest and her imitation of the consultant was fairly accurate. Melanie suppressed a smile.

'Good old Danny! And did he give you one of his famous smiles?' asked her colleague.

'You must be joking! Grave as the grave, as usual.'

The lift hesitated, dropped a couple of inches, and stopped, emptying the three midwives into the swarming ante-natal clinic. Melanie, her heart by now honestly putting in overtime, made her way as quickly as she could through the waiting area and towards the long empty corridor which housed the senior medical staff offices. At least she had not bumped into Joe. Thank heaven for small mercies, she thought, and tapped timidly on the door newly marked with an engraved plaque reading: 'Daniel Davenport FRCS, FRCOG, Consultant'. Very impressive, she thought.

As she thought it, the door opened.

'Ah—Miss Aarts! Bang on time. Shall we go?'

He whisked Melanie down towards the other end of the corridor away from the bustling clinic and down some stairs the existence of which she had never known before. This surprised her, as she knew Lessing Lane pretty well. They emerged through a side door into the doctors' car park at the back of the clinic block.

'That's handy!' she said in surprise, finding herself

being helped into the white Porsche.

'You didn't know about that escape route? How else do we obstetricians manage never to be at hand when the midwives in Ante-natal need us?'

Melanie blushed furiously. He had overheard her make this remark on their very first morning in the clinic together.

Her nerves, which had been calmed by the unexpected rush of activity, returned to their former state of tingling anxiety. She sat stiffly in the front of the Porsche, too nervous even to speculate on the torture which he had dreamed up for her today.

Dr Davenport reversed out of the parking slot with skill and speed and took them equally keenly along Lessing Lane in the direction which she had so recently driven herself.

Gradually, she became aware of his silence. His face, when she stole a look at it, had lost some of its usual rigidity and had relaxed so that she was more aware of the old sadness in it than of anything else.

'Aren't you going to ask where I'm taking you?'

'Well, I was wondering . . .'

'Breath of fresh country air,' he explained: a scant enough explanation, but one of which Melanie felt unable to seek further clarification.

'Oh!' she said.

She sat very still, as if to move would break some magic spell that held her. The familiar streets of West London disappeared and they sped along the motorway which took them away from the city. She felt it very strange to sit next to this dehospitalised doctor, in his very smart car. She looked down unseeingly at her oatmeal-coloured jersey dress. She was glad she had at least washed her hair last night . . .

'Suits you, that non-colour. More subtle than red —for the day,' he remarked coolly.

Melanie blushed again. 'Thank you,' she responded stiffly.

They drove fast in silence for another half an hour,

then turned off the motorway into green, curved
countryside. In another moment Melanie gasped. On
either side of the road beechwoods rose in newly emerald spendour, and drifts of bluebells swept across the
earth like sapphire seas. The surgeon found a lay-by and
stopped the car.

'Not quite the bulb fields of Holland, but the best that
Britain can offer, I'm afraid. Care for a walk?'

If the sight of the woods had been wonderful, the scent
of the flowers was even better. They perfumed the air
sweetly and heavily, so that each breath one took was
heavenly. A narrow path led upwards from the road,
and the two trudged up through the wood towards the
top of the rise, where the trees thinned. From there they
could look down the furrowed hillside to a farm. Everything was very still and quiet in the spring sunshine.

'This is what I miss,' sighed Dr Davenport. He scanned the landscape before him with eyes which had quite
lost their steely quality, and yet retained their distance.

'You came up here from the West Country, didn't
you?' Melanie ventured.

'Yes. Elchester. The Mendip Hills are beautiful,
especially at this time of year . . .' He spoke as if he had
forgotten her presence. '. . . sometimes the Chilterns
remind me. I drive up here some days.'

'I expect you go back down West when you get
the time off to make it worth your while?' Melanie
speculated, gazing down into the valley.

'No, I do not!'

The ferocity of his reply momentarily stunned her.
She had completely relaxed her guard, almost forgetful
of their relationship.

'I . . . I'm sorry,' she stammered. 'I had no idea . . . '

'Shall we walk back?'

He started off back down through the wood without
her, and she had to run to catch up with him. He put his
arm out and awkwardly, almost roughly round her to
draw her level with him.

'I'm sorry I snapped,' he mumbled, and his arm was

gone from her shoulders as suddenly as it had appeared there.

She consoled her bruised feelings with the wonder of the woods, storing it up in her memory. She did not remember having walked in woods like this since she was a child. She walked slowly beside the consultant, no longer even trying to make sense of this mysterious outing.

He opened the car door for her, then got in himself and reached into the back seat. He produced a packet and two apples. Unpacking the sandwiches, he laid them out on the paper on Melanie's knees.

'Two cheese and two pâté. Sorry, but you'll have to share my lunch. We'll be late if we try to get some anywhere now.'

Melanie was perfectly happy to share his lunch, and said so.

She passed his sandwiches to him as he drove, in an oddly familiar procedure which gave her pleasure, and they had bitten into their apples before he spoke again.

'I've been looking at the ultra-sound pictures on Julia Young again,' he said.

'Oh, yes?' Melanie focused on the motorway as if that symbolised her attention to work.

'She's definitely thirty-two weeks this week, and it's a big baby . . .'

'Yes,' interrupted Melanie, 'I know. I was sure she was a week on. It's a good job we came to you . . .'

'. . . as I was saying, it's a big child: forty-five centimetres long already. There's not an abnormal amount of amniotic fluid taking up the space in there. It's all baby. If he hasn't managed to turn himself around by today, I doubt I'll be able to do it.'

Melanie felt a pang of annoyance at his defeatist attitude. And another at her childish previous interruption. The discussion of Julia Young's case had caught her unawares and she was not psychologically prepared for it as she had been earlier. She knew that only four per cent of babies remained breech presentations, although they nearly all sat like that up until thirty-two weeks. She was

thinking how, oh, how could Julia's baby be one of only
four per cent?

'But you'll still try?' she asked.

'Of course. Under a general anaesthetic, if that's what
she wants. And if you agree, naturally,' he added
graciously.

'Naturally!' said Melanie. 'It's Mrs Young's wishes
that matter most to me, Dr Davenport—and her baby's
well-being, of course.'

'Of course,' he echoed. 'I couldn't agree more. And
your priorities are mine too.'

Melanie glanced at him, but there was no trace of
sarcasm in his face. Neither had there been malice in his
voice. Still, she couldn't help wondering whether the
pronouncement over the outcome of this afternoon's
visit had been purely objective.

'Contrary to your suspicions, Miss Aarts, I too respect
the right of women to choose their own care. One is
simply . . .' He seemed to choose his words with care,
'more cautious in some circumstances than in other, less
. . . complicated ones.'

'I agree,' said Melanie. 'But that's why we're coming
to Lessing Lane this afternoon. I've always said that
medical intervention and advice . . .'

'All right, Melanie, this is no time for riding hobby-
horses,' cut in the consultant coldly. 'Let's just agree
that we both want the best for this particular patient
—just as we do for others.'

Melanie nodded in silence. She felt dangerously
emotional.

The remainder of the journey back to Lessing Lane
was completed without either saying another word, and
by the time they got back, Melanie was calm again.

They climbed the back stairs again and the heat and
hubbub of the hospital assailed them pitilessly. It was to
Melanie as if the sweet woods full of bluebells and
birdsong suddenly belonged to another world.

'Hello there, you two!' Julia Young greeted them
heartily. She had been shown into the consultant's office

where she had waited for them. 'Sarah put me in here, Daniel. She said this was the only comfortable chair in the hospital.' She looked from the consultant to Melanie and back again with amusement. 'Good timing, getting here together,' she observed.

'You're very cheerful, Mrs Young,' rejoined Dr Davenport soberly.

'It's a nice day,' she explained. Her voice dropped a little. 'He's still upside down, if that's what you're moping about, Daniel.'

She smiled sweetly at his shocked glance.

Melanie controlled her own face only with difficulty. She felt a bit sorry for the consultant in his valiant attempts to keep his professional distance. But Julia really was irresistible.

'How are you feeling?' he asked softly.

'Fine!'

The three went into the consulting room next door and Melanie shut the door quietly behind them. When Julia had undressed and was up on the examination couch, Melanie pressed her hand. Julia lifted her eyebrows in an expression of resignation. She seemed very relaxed.

Dr Davenport gently palpated her abdomen.

'Yes, still sitting up the wrong way, I'm afraid,' he murmured to himself. 'Now, what's this? Ah, yes, an elbow, I think.'

He murmured and palpated for some time, so that even Melanie was taken by surprise to notice that he was exerting gentle pressure to push the baby up on one side of the uterus and gentle traction on the head to pull it down the other. As she watched his hands moving, working firmly on the taut abdomen, she saw the form beneath it slowly and unmistakably rotate.

To distract herself, she thought frantically about the Sister Tutor in the School of Midwifery telling them all that ECV had helped reduce the incidence of breech presentation from four to less than one per cent . . . and just as she realised that she was holding her breath,

Daniel Davenport stepped up to the head of the couch.

'Sit up, if you will, Mrs Young. We'll ask Sarah to get you a cup of coffee, then check that he's still where I've just put him after that.'

'You've turned him? You darling! You miracle, Daniel!'

Daniel looked quickly away, but not before Melanie had caught the corner of his smile. She helped Julia to sit up, her own heart turning somersaults in celebration. The two women grinned at one another like a couple of accomplices in a successful bank robbery.

'And good for Malcolm's best brandy!' Julia whispered to Melanie, although Daniel had gone next door to see his secretary.

'Julia! So that's why you were so cheerful! But I thought you were a firm teetotaller.'

'I am. But I was going to be calm if it killed me. It nearly did,' she grimaced at the memory of the taste.

'How much did you have?' asked Melanie.

'An eggcup-full. Ugh!'

Melanie forgot all her professional distance and forgot all about Julia being Professor Young's wife. She hugged her.

'You're amazing!' she smiled. 'And so's Dr Davenport,' she added reverently.

'But I bet you don't tell him that,' said Julia, with a significant sidelong look at Melanie.

'I will if your baby's still the right way up in ten minutes' time,' she promised.

But when it came to it, those weren't exactly the words that came to mind.

'Thank you very much, Dr Davenport,' she said as they left, 'for everything.'

He surveyed her coolly and saved his smile for her client.

'Very well, Miss Aarts. Mrs Young. Take care. And goodbye.'

In spite of his earlier assurances, Melanie got the distinct impression that he did not altogether share their joy.

CHAPTER SEVEN

As soon as Julia had gone off in her own direction and Melanie was heading back towards the practice, her elation began to fade and she began to think.

Obviously, whatever it was that Dr Davenport had wanted to talk to her about, the reason had evaporated by today. He had covered himself by taking her along on one of his customary, but usually solitary, lunchtime outings from the hospital.

She could not help connecting this with his obvious earlier conviction that he would not be able to turn Julia's baby, and the coldness of his manner directly he had proved himself wrong. All this pointed to the fact that he continued to distrust her with Julia's care.

As if this wasn't enough for her to have to live with, she had managed to touch him on a particularly raw spot with her chatter during their walk. She recoiled inside at the memory. And yet how could she have known? She knew nothing about him.

As usual, she decided to bury her confused feelings in a surfeit of work. The practice came to her aid, producing a burst of deliveries and new clients.

One morning, in a booking clinic, the consultant's assertion that he believed in a woman's right to choose returned to her. Even if he thinks I'm a rotten midwife, she thought wildly, he can't possibly blame me for seducing Julia Young into a foolish choice. I didn't even know the woman before she presented herself to me.

That evening at around nine, she was settling down with her book in the flat—Rachel was out as usual—when the telephone rang. Melanie was alert and half ready to dash out of the house, as she always was when on call. One of her clients told her that she was in early labour, having contractions every fifteen or twenty minutes which were lasting much longer than the familiar Braxton Hicks'.

Melanie went back to her book, thanking heaven for good ante-natal education which gave midwives the chance of some solid sleep before a delivery. The call gave her ample warning of an early morning delivery for a prima gravida, first babies rarely arriving in much less than twelve hours.

Sure enough, the next call was at half past five, and Melanie was ready for it, in her typical on-call half-sleep. She got up, dressed and went out into the chilly dawn. She loved this time of day, shared only with the first birds, the city streets deserted and tranquil.

The baby arrived at five to eight after a simple and uncomplicated second stage. Melanie had the satisfaction of seeing the couple share the birth of their son, and she left them as soon as she had finished her work, to share their joy in privacy. As always, the birth left her with a sense of wonder at the world, looking with fresh pleasure at the schoolchildren, the neat commuters and the shopgirls who had each arrived so naked and defenceless in this world.

She worked the day through at the practice and went home to bed early to try to catch up on her sleep. It was Friday night and somebody was holding a party nearby. She lay awake, watching the sweep of headlights of passing cars across the ceiling, listening to the distant music, laughter and voices in the street.

Everybody seemed to be out having fun. And here was she, twenty-seven, single and rapidly turning into a workaholic. She told herself not to be quite so stupid and pathetic. For some reason she thought of how Julia Young had been thirty before she had married Professor Young. And one of the most dedicated Sisters at Lessing Lane, according to Rachel, who had been recounting gossip, unsuspecting of her flatmate's special interest in such things. It seemed that the Young romance had been the talk of Lessing Lane for months after it had been made public, and a great deal longer before.

Apparently, Malcolm Young had been quite a dish in his day, and a dark horse too: a potent mixture. Watch as they might, the midwives had been unable to attach his name to anyone, and Julia Marchmont had been the last person they'd have suspected. They thought of her as a typical ex-Army nursing Sister whose frustrated maternal instinct had turned her into a midwife. And nothing would budge her from Labour until she was given honourable discharge.

Well, they'd been wrong. And not for the first time, nor presumably the last. Grapevines often yielded dud fruit, especially hospital grapevines. Too much inbreeding; too little hard pruning back, Melanie reflected. She recalled what Rachel had said about Daniel Davenport; 'No news there, I'm afraid—The Man With No Past. Mind you, I don't suppose that matters too much if your future looks as rosy as his does. Tipped for the chair after Prof. Young. And if the rumours are right about the Prof. considering an overseas appointment for a time, that might make old dour Danny the youngest Professor of Obs and Gynae in London. Probably Europe. He's certainly got the brains for the job, but he might have to work on his bedside manner!'

Melanie remembered her cool lack of interest in this story, and the silence she had kept about his bedside manner. She knew his way with patients lacked nothing. She made up for her discretion with Rachel, by wildly imagining Daniel Davenport as a Professor. He would be different from Prof. Young, but just as close to his patients and people, she decided. For some reason, she did not touch on his manner with members of the midwifery staff, but concentrated instead on the brilliance of his academic career.

She closed her eyes. The picture of a woman floated into her mind, a woman with a familiar, unplaceable face—the woman at the Ball. Melanie opened her eyes as if to face the truth. This was the face of the new Professor's wife . . .

A crash of broken glass through an unopened window

nearby broke in on her thoughts. It was followed by the burst of laughter and the sound of voices raised in hilarity. When things quietened down, Melanie drifted into sleep.

It seemed only seconds later that she was awoken by the ringing telephone. Blearily, she saw that it was one a.m.

'Every five minutes? I'll be over as soon as I can, Amy. Just carry on as you've been taught to do. No, of *course* it's no bother!'

Of all Melanie's current clients, only Amy James could apologise for the 'bother' after completing half of first stage quite unaided. Amy was an unmarried mother by choice. A shy, diffident woman whose outer appearance belied her tough self-sufficiency, she had endeared herself to Melanie with her longing for her unborn baby. Strange and unapproachable at first, she reminded Melanie of a beautiful cat: independent and secretive, yet the most gentle and responsive of friends.

Amy was well advanced into first stage by the time Melanie got to her tiny, pretty flat. She had left the front door unlocked for Melanie, and Melanie slipped quietly in, calling her own name as she did so. She went into Amy's bedroom. In the corner of it stood an old-fashioned wicker crib. It had been exquisitely lined and frilled by hand with soft, printed cotton, and was freshly made up.

'I've put a hot water bottle in the cot . . . ooh!' whispered Amy.

'Let's see how you're getting on,' said Melanie.

She took off her coat and rolled up the sleeves of her dress. Putting on a plastic disposable apron, she opened her bag and washed her hands at the spotless sink in the bedroom. In the mirror as she did so, she watched the reflection of her client, breathing faithfully through her contractions.

Melanie did a quick check; everything was ready. There were plenty of clean soft towels and all the first requirements for the baby, checked at the last ante-natal

visit she had made. The room was warm. There was a
clean bucket for disposables and another for soiled linen,
bedblocks to raise the bed if Amy's blood pressure
should drop, a bedpan and plastic sheeting as well as
incontinence pads and maternity towels.

Everything else she had brought with her in her
delivery pack: sterile supplies, gloves, syringes, drugs,
umbilical clamp and plastic clips, sutures and so on. She
was confident she was ready for the birth.

Amy lay quite still while she examined her.

'That's wonderful, Amy. You're nearly there—six
centimetres.'

Amy did not reply, but concentrated on the next
contraction. They were coming every three minutes
now. In between, Melanie checked Amy's pulse and
blood pressure and carefully palpated and listened to the
baby's heart.

She knew that all was well with the baby. She had
noted the cephalic presentation: a small caput or normal
swelling of the baby's head during labour, through the
dilated cervix, or neck of the womb. Although small in
stature, Amy was blessed with an ample pelvis, and
Melanie could foresee no cause for difficulty in the
coming delivery.

Amy suddenly relaxed for a moment and then went
without delay into second stage. Melanie adjusted her
position on the bed, placing pillows behind her head so
as make her most comfortable to push. She worked hard
and well, often managing three pushes per contraction,
and Melanie soon delivered the small, dark head of her
child.

After a moment's rest, the first shoulder was born and
Melanie gave the routine injection of ergometrine 0.5
mg that would aid contraction of the uterus after the
birth of the baby, and expulsion of the afterbirth. And
then it was all over.

'It's a boy,' Melanie announced quietly.

Tears were running down Amy's face. They were
strangely incompatible with her ecstatic smile—like a

rainbow in a stormy sky.

'Oh, Melanie, I can't believe it. I can't believe it!' she kept repeating, stroking her son. Smeary and travel-weary as he was, he looked very like his little dark-haired mother.

A moment or so later Melanie divided him off from her and he gave a lusty cry, turning bright pink from head to toe as he did so.

It was odd, but suddenly the little flat seemed quite full of people. The three of them seemed to generate such a confusion of activity, although in fact, Amy was lying quietly while Melanie attended first to the baby and then to her. Jason and then Amy were bathed and dressed in fresh things, and the baby was soon sleeping in his crib beside his mother's bed.

'Melanie, just before you go, would you mind very much telephoning my friend David for me? He didn't want to be here for the birth, I know, but now . . . he made me promise I'd phone as soon as his son was born! And he can do all the other ritual telephoning to broadcast the good news.' Amy smiled shyly, 'He's a journalist,' she explained.

Melanie was relieved. She had been about to ask whom she should ask to come, as Amy could not get up to the bathroom for at least ten hours and there was always a danger of post-partum haemorrhage.

'I'd be glad to ring. And I'm not leaving until he arrives,' she said.

When he did, it was difficult to tell who he was most proud of: Amy or Jason. And he was full of gratitude to Melanie, which she hardly felt she deserved.

Although only a few hours had passed since last she was in the street, a pearly grey dawn was lighting the sky and Melanie felt as if days had gone by. She realised that it was Saturday and that she could go straight back to bed. But her excitement over the birth she had just witnessed would, she knew, prevent her from sleeping straight away.

She drove home and let herself quietly in. Back in her

warm bed, she read for a little while, then fell into a
dreamless sleep.

If ninety-five per cent of women are superstitious, then a
hundred per cent of nurses and midwives are! Melanie
was perfectly prepared to be called out again that night.
She had slept long and deep until early afternoon, and
been awoken by Rachel with a cup of welcome tea. She
told Rachel she was expecting another call.

'Bound to come,' agreed Rachel cheerfully. 'When do
they not arrive in threes?'

The two girls nevertheless went out together to do the
weekend household shopping, Melanie's bleep in her
pocket. They got involved in a long and fruitless search
for cord trousers for Rachel, who was very choosy about
the cut.

'Men's ones are the best for that,' asserted Melanie, as
Rachel discarded a fourth pair of trousers over the top of
the changing cubicle with a hiss that heralded a swear-
word.

She emerged, pink-faced, a second later.

'That's all right for you,' she eyed Melanie's long slim
legs and slim hips with envy, 'but less helpful if you're
built like an attenuated stick insect—like myself.'

Melanie smiled. 'I seem to recall glances cast in your
direction that cast doubt on that description,' she said.

They let themselves back into the flat and put down
their shopping bags with relief. Rachel put the kettle on
and they unpacked everything.

'You'll never guess what—I'm free tonight!' she
announced, as if surprised herself, 'How about a film?'

'Is everything all right?' asked Melanie in mock
horror.

Rachel laughed.

'Toby's gone home to see his parents and prepare
them for a visit from me: the Steady Girl-friend,' she
explained. 'And then he's got a worse job: to prepare me
for it. His father's a retired Army surgeon and Mummy's
an ex-Matron QARANC. Ugh!'

'Queen Alexandra's Royal Army Nursing Corps!' Melanie, pouring tea, saluted with her free hand. 'I've always had a secret passion for them. It's those lovely bright red capes, I think. They look like *real* nurses. What rank would a Matron be? A General?'

'Goodness knows,' Rachel shivered. 'Something terrifying like that. I'll tell you when I know.'

'Don't bother,' laughed Melanie, 'I'll ask her myself at the wedding!'

Rachel coloured. It was interesting to see the boot on the other foot, and Melanie said so.

'I'm going to have a bath,' she added. 'Will you choose the film? You're the expert these days.'

They went to see a Woody Allen film that made them both cry with laughter. Afterwards, they treated themselves to a curry in the New Bombay Restaurant which, they agreed, was even better than their local place which supplied them with their weekly carry-out at ridiculously cheap prices.

'It's because they work so hard,' said Melanie, and told Rachel a little about Amina Chowdhary.

In the middle of the night she was awoken by the telephone and, still struggling to make sense of the world, thought she must be dreaming when she heard Amina's voice.

'Amina?'

'Please, I am very sorry to ring you. But I am bleeding now.'

Melanie looked at her clock. It was three a.m.

'Amina,' she said quietly, 'go back to bed and stay there. I'm coming now. Don't worry about the baby. Everything will be okay.'

Melanie was now wide awake. She dressed quickly, her mind already occupied with the task ahead. Amina was twenty-nine weeks pregnant. The most likely cause of ante-partum haemorrhage at this stage was placenta praevia. The condition demanded hospitalisation because the bleeding was almost certain to continue or to recur up until delivery, and certainly during it. Although placenta praevia was rare, occurring only about once in every hundred pregnancies, it was commoner than any of the other causes of ante-partum haemorrhage.

Melanie grabbed her bag and left the flat. She drove as quickly and safely as she could through the deserted streets and past the usual couple of remaindered drunken carousers. Amina lived fifteen minutes from Bedford Park.

She rang the doorbell and was immediately admitted by a worried husband.

'Hello, Mr Chowdhary,' Melanie smiled calmly.

'Please. This way.'

The bedroom was softly lit and Amina looked even more fragile than usual, sitting up in the big, perfectly-made bed. A tall grey-haired woman in a yellow sari hovered near the bed, shaking her head. Melanie greeted her formally, then asked her to leave the room while she examined Amina.

'I think you'd be better staying lying down,' she concluded.

The frightened look in Amina's eyes faded as Melanie's familiar thorough examination proceeded. Amina's blood pressure was within normal limits and she was not clinically shocked. Her pulse was rapid, but full and strong. She had not lost too much blood.

'I'm afraid I shall have to find you a bed in the hospital, Amina,' Melanie said gently. 'We must find out exactly why you've been bleeding, and hospital is the best place for you.' She took Amina's hand. 'It's possible that the doctor will want to keep you in until your baby is born, Amina,' she said.

Amina regarded her solemnly. She thought for some time. 'If it has to be so,' she said at last.

Melanie reassured her about the baby, certain it would not come to harm and would be delivered safely.

Perhaps, she thought, the idea of hospital was not so unpleasant to Amina. Perhaps it would be the best place for her to rest until the birth. Amina lay back calmly, and Melanie went to the living room. She explained to Amina's husband and mother-in-law what was happening, then dialled Lessing Lane.

'The Admitting Medical Officer, please.'

There was a short pause.

'Davenport here.'

'Dr Davenport? Melanie Aarts. I've a patient for you: twenty-nine weeks, prima gravida, query placenta praevia with moderate bleeding of an hour's duration. Maternal pulse and blood pressure are normal and the baby's heart rate is normal. She's at rest. There are no other obvious causes for immediate concern. Will you admit her, please?'

'There'll be a bed ready for her on Lister and I'll be up to see her as soon as she's in,' he confirmed briskly. 'What's her name?' A pause. 'Okay.'

The telephone went dead.

'We'll go in in my car. It's quicker than calling an ambulance, and you can come with us, Mr Chowdhary,' Melanie said kindly.

Amina was got up and wrapped in a warm dressing gown. Melanie supervised the quick collection of essentials to take with them and Amina was soon tucked cosily into the back seat of Melanie's car in a blanket, her husband beside her. They were at Lessing Lane in ten minutes. Melanie got them swiftly up to the ante-natal ward, and Night Sister met them in the doorway.

'Ah, Midwife Aarts—back with us so soon! And Mrs Chowdhary? Now, my dear, we've a nice warm bed waiting for you!'

Two pupil midwives appeared and Sister vanished.

Amina was helped out of the wheelchair which Melanie had commandeered for her at the front door and her patient was taken out of her hands. Melanie was left standing at the station in the middle of the ward.

As usual, she was assailed by the overwhelming femininity of a ward full of women; the smells of talcum powders and colognes, flowers and fresh linen. And as usual, something deep inside her responded to it all and it was all she could do to stop herself taking off her coat, sitting down here at the top of the ward and reading the Kardex. If a patient had rung her bell, she knew her legs would carry her swiftly and unhesitatingly to her bedside.

'Hello, Melanie! How's tricks?'

It was Joyce Hills, a senior staff midwife of her own set who had left Lessing Lane when she got married three years before.

'What are *you* doing here?' Melanie asked in surprise.

'Couldn't stay away. Being a kept woman's not for me,' Joyce grinned, 'and anyway, I got withdrawal symptoms.'

Melanie thought about her own feelings about the ward.

'I know what you mean,' she said. 'Have you been on nights since you came back, or are you relieving?'

'No. Just nights up here on Lister. I love it, and Peter's a policeman doing night shift too this year, so it suits us fine. We just live the other way up from most other people! Ah, here's our Danny boy, up to see your patient, I presume. Good morning, Dr Davenport.'

He glanced at the ward clock, which said four-thirty a.m., and glowered at Joyce, then generously extended the glower to include Melanie.

'Where is she?' he demanded to know.

'Left four,' said Joyce, indicating the screened bed. As he turned away she gave Melanie a grim smile. 'Charming chap,' she whispered. 'A real early riser!'

As the tall broad figure of the consultant went through the screens, one of the pupil midwives emerged, leaving the more senior to chaperon him. The pupil who had left Amina went straight out to talk to her husband in the corridor and give him a cup of tea.

Meanwhile, Joyce gave Melanie a seat, and Melanie proceeded to give Joyce a thorough report on Amina's history and present condition. Joyce scribbled notes while she did so.

'Probably keep her in until term, even if she stops

bleeding—if she goes that far. Danny's a stickler on placenta praevias, and so's the Prof., if you recall. Still, at least he's not so handy with his knife as some I could mention. Do you remember old Soames—"Slasher Soames"—did Caesars like other people drink tea?'

Melanie did remember him, the old consultant from their training days. She shivered at the memory and Joyce nodded as Daniel Davenport approached the station with a set face.

'Very well, her husband can go in now. You were correct in your diagnosis, Miss Aarts.' He turned swiftly to Joyce. 'Placenta praevia. Complete bedrest. No shock. Half-hourly recordings, please. I've written her up for Valium twenty-five milligrams stat, and more four-hourly prn—that should keep her calm. I'll see her again in the morning. If her BP drops or she starts bleeding again ring me. Miss Aarts, I'll have a word with you outside.'

Melanie followed him into the darkened ward corridor. He stowed the tubes of blood he had just taken from Amina into his white coat pocket.

'I want to keep her in,' he said. 'The bleeding's not too bad, but if it continues she'll have to stay in bed. Even if we can have a spontaneous delivery, I'll want to rupture the membranes myself.' He stopped abruptly, evidently expecting her to speak.

'Fine, Dr Davenport. I'm very happy that she's safely in your hands. I've explained the possibility that she might have to be admitted for the rest of the pregnancy, and I think she and her husband both accept that.'

Daniel Davenport's face relaxed.

'So we'll just have to see how we go from here,' he said briskly.

'Indeed. May I go and see Mrs Chowdhary now? If you've finished with me?'

'Certainly. Oh, and Miss Aarts . . . Mrs Chowdhary seemed—er—anxious that you would be able to attend the delivery, even though it will take place here. Of course, I assured her that that would be possible.' Even in the dim light of the corridor, Melanie made out a softening in his features, a twitch in his jaw as he subdued a smiled. 'She appears to be rather attached to you. Absolute trust, that sort of thing . . .'

'Really?' Melanie met his eyes with mild surprise. 'That's odd, isn't it Dr Davenport? Still, it takes all sorts . . .'

Several times over the next two or three weeks Melanie thought how strange it had been to have seen the consultant at all the night she had taken Amina in. He was much too senior to do regular stints as an admitting officer; even Joe Peters covered only when there were too few junior doctors to do so.

Then she remembered that it was early summer already, and the beginning of the holiday season. It was amazing how quickly she had slipped out of habitual hospital thinking. Joe was probably taking an early holiday so that he would be around to cover for the registrars doing the Fellowship exams soon, and Dr Davenport would be covering for Joe. On reflection, Melanie decided that a brush with the consultant was marginally more acceptable than one with Joe Peters. But the thought of prolonged and regular contact with the consultant over Amina gave her an uncomfortable sensation in the pit of her stomach.

She'd coped well with it so far. Visiting Amina a couple of times a week, she had managed to time them so as to avoid meeting him. He did his rounds between nine and twelve each alternate morning, and Melanie knew when his routine operating lists were. The only thing she could not cater for were his emergency and surprise arrivals on the ward.

Having officially handed over the care of her client to the staff at Lessing Lane, Melanie restricted herself to a purely supportive role, reinforcing the treatment which Amina received and encouraging her trust in the system. She didn't need too much encouragement. Amina had taken to the ward like a duck to water, enjoying being among so many women and able to make new friends outside her rather restricted family circle.

It was a Tuesday, three weeks after Amina's admission, that Julia Young appeared at the practice for the last time. Bridget had made it standard practice to see clients at their home after the thirty-sixth week of pregnancy. This gave them desirable relief from the journey to the ante-natal clinic, and the midwives a chance to acclimatise themselves to the place where the birth would be.

Julia heaved herself up on to the examination couch with some difficulty.

'This is when I wish I was eighteen,' she puffed. 'Twenty years must make quite a difference at this stage.'

'It doesn't seem to,' replied Melanie. 'Eight or nine kilos of water and baby take their toll however old Mum is. I've seen plenty of twenty-year-olds take longer than you just have to climb up there at this stage.'

'Melanie, you're a tonic!'

Melanie checked that the baby was still head down in its cephalic presentation. It was now making its way apparently uneventfully towards full term.

At the pressure from her foetal heart monitor, the room was filled with the vigorous sound of the baby's heartbeat, and mother and midwife exchanged smiles of satisfaction.

'I'm getting very excited,' admitted Julia, her eyes shining.

'I'll tell you a secret,' said Melanie, 'so am I!'

She had so often felt like this in anticipation of a birth when some sort of special bond had formed between herself and the mother-to-be. But this was something new: this sense of total involvement. Melanie had never felt able so freely to express it.

Julia got down from the couch and lowered herself into a chair. Melanie dipped a test stick into the sample of urine she had brought with her and read the negative findings.

'That's fine,' she confirmed, 'and so's your weight gain. No swelling of your ankles or hands?'

'Well, I've had to take my rings off,' admitted Julia, 'but it's nothing really. They just get tight in the evening and then by the morning I can get them on again.'

It was a common enough complaint, and easily distinguishable from the gross swelling and true fluid retention of pre-eclampsia, the high blood pressure syndrome which could threaten a pregnancy.

Melanie tightened the sphyg cuff around Julia's upper arm and pumped the mercury up to the top of the column. Applying her stethoscope over the pulsing artery, Melanie gradually deflated the cuff and listened. There was a slight rise, but it was not significant—yet. But it was enough to alert Melanie.

She folded the cuff neatly away in the box. 'Your BP's up just a tiny bit, Julia. Take things easy, and I'll come and see you next week. You're not having any headaches, are you?'

'Haven't had one in years,' asserted Julia. 'But I'll put my feet up a bit, I promise you.'

At least Julia wasn't worried. And that was a good sign. As soon as she had gone and Bridget was free, she told her about the blood pressure.

'No protein in her urine, and no proper ankle swelling?'

'No.'

'She'll be okay, Melanie. Keep a close eye, though. Today must have been her last visit here?'

'That's right.'

'The closer she gets to term, the more you'll worry. And poor Amina hasn't helped your state of mind. Go home and have a nice hot bath and relax. Nothing's going to go wrong for your precious Baby Young!'

'I hope not,' replied Melanie.

'I was just like you with my first patient,' Bridget assured her partner, 'and she gave birth to a lovely baby girl in four hours flat. You can imagine who was most nervous at the delivery!'

Melanie did as Bridget had told her to do. She lay in the bath and breathed in the perfume of pine bath salts, luxuriating in the cloudy, silken water.

Rachel was working a late shift at Lessing Lane, and the flat was a haven of peace. Melanie lay and dreamed until the water cooled, then got out and slipped into a fresh nightdress and her wrap; there was no point in getting dressed again. She settled down to read for the evening.

Rachel came in at ten, and the two gossiped for an hour, then went to bed. The telephone rang almost immediately.

'It's for you, Mella,' called Rachel, having picked up the instrument on her way from the bathroom to her own room. 'Daniel!' she added with a cheeky grin.

'I'm taking Amina Chowdhary to theatre,' the consultant announced as soon as she picked up the receiver. 'We should get her down there for midnight—no point waiting for a spontaneous delivery with these persistent bleeders. Are you coming in?'

'Yes.' Melanie collected herself. 'Thank you for notifying me, Dr Davenport.'

He had hung up.

Melanie took pity on her hovering flatmate. 'One of my clients—he's going to do a Caesar on her, and he's invited me along to watch.'

'Nice of him,' said Rachel with amusement. 'Very sweet! Well, have a nice time,' and she trotted off to bed.

Joyce Hills welcomed Melanie's appearance on Lister with a warm smile. 'She'll be so pleased to see you, bless her,' she said, nodding towards Amina's screened bed.

'How is she?'

'A bit nervous. She's been bleeding ever since we admitted her, though, then quite heavily in the last twenty-four hours. She's had nil by mouth since lunch-time, poor love, when they first thought they might take her to theatre. Then they've been dithering about whether to give her a general or not, so she's had atropine and an antacid, which is all she's getting as a pre-med. They cross-matched her for blood about two. She's been prepped and they're just getting her ready for theatre now. Her husband's on his way in.'

Melanie took hold of Amina's hand. She looked very young and defenceless in the big white theatre gown, her beautiful long black hair concealed beneath a paper mobcap. The atropine had dilated her pupils, making her eyes seem larger than ever.

'So you're going to have your baby tonight, Amina. Isn't that lovely? And your husband is coming to see you.'

'Yes,' whispered Amina.

'And in an hour or so you'll be back in your bed and the baby will be safe and sound in the nursery.'

'It is so quick?'

'Very quick, Amina. And you won't feel any pain.'

Amina's eyes sought Melanie's. The fear left them.

'Now, are you going to tell me what names you've chosen? Or is it a secret?'

Two equally tall and gangly theatre attendants arrived with a trolley and Amina was gently lifted on to it. Melanie walked beside the trolley all the way to the theatre, talking softly now and then to her client.

'Hello again, Mrs Chowdhary,' said Bob Daley, the anaesthetist, heartily. 'Now, are you going to let Melanie here go and change, or does she have to come into our nice clean theatre with her coat on?'

Ten minutes later, showered and in theatre gear, Melanie was standing beside the operating table. Next to her, Amina was being draped with sterile green towels. A screen of towels had already been erected over a frame across her chest, so that although she was to remain awake, she could not see her own abdomen.

At the back of the operating theatre stood an incubator and a trolley set with resuscitation equipment for the baby. Melanie hoped she would not need it. The child should be perfectly viable by now and the delivery should go smoothly. Apart from the presence of the incubator, the theatre might have been set up for any surgical procedure.

'Well, we finally decided on an epidural, didn't we, Mrs Chowdhary,' Bob smiled at his patient over his mask, 'in spite of the advanced stage of starvation and the pre-med. Never mind, Mrs Chowdhary, we'll give you a nice cup of tea and a couple of special sandwiches after this.' He began to introduce local anaesthetic into the polythene catheter which he had positioned in the lumbar region of the spinal cord.

'Here you are, Melanie—a ringside seat.' He drew a high stool forward. From it, Melanie could both watch the forthcoming operation and comfort Amina.

Melanie had never seen Daniel Davenport in theatre before, and the effect of the mask was surprising. For the first time she seemed to see the true intensity of the blue eyes and the total concentration of his attention in them. She saw too, for the first time, tiny laughter lines at their corners and, under the remorseless light from the operating lamp, signs of tiredness and sleepless nights too. For a split second Melanie envied the Theatre Sister who, as if in response to her thought, sighed and stepped closer to the surgeon, awaiting his first decision. She held the scalpel.

'Pfannenstiel, I think, eh, Sister? Altogether more aesthetically pleasing, these transverse incisions.' A little louder, for the benefit of Amina, he added, 'You won't be able to see the scar at all in a month or two, down below the bikini line.'

The scalpel was placed in his hand.

Melanie smiled reassuringly at Amina above their masks. Amina's hand dampened and tightened on her own, but the brown eyes remained calm.

Swiftly and deftly and now in silence, Dr Davenport set to work, and in no time at all a little dark head appeared as if by magic beneath his hands. He delivered the head, wrinkled and grimacing. Melanie held her breath as Sister swiftly wiped the mouth, nose and eyes clean with a sterile swab and sucked the mucus out of its

nose and mouth. Then the rest of the baby was gently
lifted out and held upside down. Melanie saw Daniel
Davenport's eyes soften unmistakably above the mask.

He's a born surgeon, thought Melanie. She had never
seen a more impressive Caesarean section. It had taken
precisely seven minutes so far.

A thin high cry broke the silence of the operating
theatre, then a louder yell as Sister took hold of the
baby.

'Oh, Amina, it's a little boy!' breathed Melanie.

Uncomprehension, then realisation, then joy replaced one another in Amina's eyes. She stared at the
little wriggling pink form held high in Sister's hands for
her to see.

'A little boy,' she repeated.

'Congratulations, Mrs Chowdhary,' boomed Dr
Davenport. 'Well done, Bob!'

'We did all right, didn't we, Mrs Chowdhary, in our
modest little way.' He stroked his patient's forehead
gently.

Melanie took the baby. He scored well on his Apgar,
by which she tested his vital functions in the minutes
immediately following birth. He did not require any
resuscitation. She stood by while the paediatrician who
had arrived in theatre examined him, then put him in the
incubator ready for transferral for routine observation
to the Special Care Baby Unit.

'He's a lovely healthy baby, Amina. Really beautiful!'
she told her.

It was another forty minutes before the surgeon had
tidied his patient up.

'There we are, Mrs Chowdhary,' he said. 'That wasn't
too bad, now was it?'

Amina opened her eyes and thanked him sleepily. She
had been resting quietly for the past half hour or so,
while Melanie sat beside her and Bob Daley maintained
a good level of local anaesthetic.

'All over!' said Melanie.

Downstairs, she whispered a last good night to

Amina, whose husband had just come back up to the ward from the SCBU where he had seen his son for the first time.

'And good night to you too, Joyce,' said Melanie as she passed the station. Hardly a patient had stirred while Amina was being lifted gently back to bed.

'I'll be sorry to lose her to Post-natal tomorrow,' said Joyce. 'She's been the light of the ward, our Amina.'

'I hope she's made lots of real friends,' said Melanie.

Outside the ward the very bricks and mortar of the old maternity hospital seemed to sleep. The corridors echoed emptily as Melanie walked softly and quickly to the stairs. She could not face the lift tonight. All her pent-up energy and excitement had made her edgy. It was better to be scrubbed up for a Caesarean, she decided, than to be a passive onlooker. She stepped down the stairs two at a time, wondering how she would ever get to sleep when she got home.

'What are you doing, Miss Aarts? Practising for the Olympics? Trying to tire yourself out?'

Daniel Davenport surveyed her as she descended the last couple of stairs. He was leaning against the wall in the main corridor, beneath a muted night light. He looked as if he was in a 1930s gangster film: very laconic, very laid-back. And he was smiling.

'The lift's so noisy . . .' she began, confused. For some reason, he was the last person she had expected to see again tonight.

'Do you spend *all* your time thinking about other people?' he enquired conversationally.

'No, it wasn't that . . .'

'Well, *I* was just thinking of offering *you* a lift home,' he told her.

'But I've got my own car outside . . .'

'In that case, I'll walk you to it. Walk, mind you, not run. I'm bloody exhausted, even if you're not.'

'That was a beautiful Caesar,' remarked Melanie. She did not really know what to say to him at this hour, under these conditions. It was all very disorientating.

'She was a beautifully calm and well-prepared patient,' he returned.

Melanie registered the compliment, but could not respond to it. The consultant opened the back door into the car park and a rush of cold air met them. He walked beside her to her car.

When they reached it, he put his arms around her and kissed her capably and calmly, as if it were a regular event. His relaxation lent a sureness to his touch and a sensuality to his kiss which Melanie had never imagined, let alone experienced. He did not hold her hard or close, and she could have broken free of him at any time. But she stayed in his embrace knowing that he knew she did not resist him. He kissed her long and slowly, then let her go, holding her away from him, a hand on each of her shoulders.

'Good night,' he said. 'Sleep well.' A muscle twitched in his cheek.

Melanie felt her legs shaking. The moment he let her go she dived into her car, reversed out of the car park and sped down Lessing Lane as though her life depended upon making her escape.

What was he doing to her? She was incoherent with emotion. What was that for? she thought. He's perfectly charming to me the minute he's chivalrously relieved me of responsibility for one of my own patients! Damned doctor, she thought. Male chauvinist pig!

But something deep inside her remained unconvinced, despite her feverish attempts to rationalise that kiss.

CHAPTER EIGHT

BRIGHTON was beautiful. The town thrilled with summer life; birds sang in the parks and the shops hummed with lithe brown shoppers. The Pavilion shone with strangely Oriental splendour and the pier pointed its rusty finger through the sparkling waves towards France.

Melanie and Rachel wandered aimlessly and happily up and down the Lanes, exploring the little shops full of lovely old and new things. This was the middle of the second week of their holiday and London and work seemed a world away.

They moved through a treasure trove of silk scarves, amber beads and fragile Indian cotton dresses, admiring the colours and prices of things, comparing them to those they had seen elsewhere. The air smelled of sea and incense.

Rachel had just bought herself two pairs of trousers without any difficulty in finding a fit, and Melanie had got two light summer dresses for the London price of one. Rachel had had to persuade her to buy the second —a black cotton strapped dress for summer evenings which Melanie had thought too dressy.

'Try it on,' Rachel had encouraged. 'It'll look stunning!'

It had.

And now they were looking for somewhere to sit and have a cup of coffee. They found a white, palm-fronded café and, ordering, Melanie remembered the tea that she had shared with Julia not so long ago at Kew. It was the second time that morning that she had thought about it. About half an hour before she had caught her breath at a silver object in an antique shop window, but the little toy had not closely resembled the lovely Victorian teething ring that Julia had bought.

147

'If a couple of hours' shopping tires us out like this, how are we going to face work again?' she heard herself ask Rachel.

Rachel shrugged. 'God knows,' she said cheerfully. 'Retire, perhaps?'

'Could you?' asked Melanie, half serious. 'I mean, if you got married, would you?'

'If, if, if . . .' Rachel smiled.

'Well,' continued Melanie speculatively, 'I bet this is the last holiday we spend together.'

'Give us a chance, Melanie! I haven't even met the Majors yet.'

Melanie stared. 'Both of them?'

'I think so,' grinned Rachel. 'But as to your first question: yes, I think I could retire. In fact, there's nothing I'd like better. I'm tired of other people's babies. I'd like some of my own.'

This unequivocal statement of her position amazed Melanie, who had never heard her friend admit to anything remotely identifiable to a maternal instinct.

'You would?'

'Truly,' replied Rachel. 'I'd like a pretty house with a garden, so I could grow all our own vegetables . . .'

'You'd what?' exclaimed Melanie.

'Well, wouldn't you?'

'Well, I . . . I haven't thought . . .'

Rachel looked at her thoughtfully.

'You've discussed this recently with someone,' said Melanie suddenly. 'It's all tied up, decided.'

'Don't mention this to another soul, Melanie. I wasn't going to tell even you—Toby made me promise.' Rachel took a huge bite of cheesecake, while her friend stared open-mouthed at her.

'When's the wedding?'

'Christmas,' said Rachel.

'Rachel! Congratulations!'

'Thank you.'

There was a moment's silence in which the two friends grinned foolishly at one another.

'And the baby?' ventured Melanie at last.

Rachel laughed.

'Not this year, perhaps next. It's no shotgun wedding. Toby and I are neither of us patient people, but at least in some ways we're quite responsible. We'll see how we get on for a while.'

Melanie was obscurely relieved not to have to absorb more than one piece of surprise news.

'When did you decide to get married?' she asked.

'You really want to know?'

'Of course I do!'

'At the Ball.'

'The night you met?'

'Right.'

'But that only happens in novels. Are you sure? Do you know him well enough?'

Rachel sighed patiently. 'Yes and yes,' she said. 'Toby proposed during one of the last dances. It was very romantic!' Her eyes sparkled with happiness and a hint of amusement at Melanie's amazement. 'It was that woman with the beautiful velvety voice—Roberta Flack —singing *The First Time Ever I Saw Your Face*. Do you remember?'

Melanie swallowed hard.

'Yes,' she said, 'I remember.' She paused painfully, trying with all her self-control to forget Daniel's arms around her, his closeness. But suddenly the sunny day seemed suffocating. She had to stop herself from getting up and running to the beach . . . anywhere. She heard words tumbling out of her own mouth. 'But why leave it until Christmas, if you're so sure?'

'We wouldn't have done, but I have to meet the parents, and Toby's used up all his holidays for this year, taking a sailing course—before we met, of course!' laughed Rachel.

'And so I'll be carrying the lamp into old age alone,' rejoined Melanie lightly. 'Oh, well, I could do worse.'

'Joe?' asked Rachel gently. 'Has that really died a death?'

'Thoroughly,' declared Melanie. 'And with it my interest in the entire male species.' She hoped the lie was a white one. She felt in no state to discuss her secrets with Rachel today. Yet confidences seemed contagious; no sooner was one out than another was nudging its way into the open. She shut her mind and her mouth firmly.

'It's funny,' said Rachel, her head on one side appraisingly, 'but you just don't look the spinster type to me. Slim, but not untouchable; quiet, but not silent enough for the convent. No, I think you're still waiting for Mr Right.'

Melanie laughed. 'You're incorrigible, Rachel! Suffering from a frustrated imagination ever since I left Lessing Lane and you lost the chance to work openly on my disastrous love-life!'

'Oh, I don't know,' Rachel smiled happily. 'If anything, it's easier now. You've got such a limited range of male colleagues. Even more limited now!'

It was perfectly true that Toby was by far the most regular medical caller at the practice and the one with whom they worked most closely. Other general practitioners referred the odd client or liaised over her care, but it was Toby, who had been a student under Prof. Young and his faithful disciple, who really considered the practice his special place of patronage. He had loved obstetrics and gynaecology as a student, but not quite enough to pursue a hospital career for them. He made up for that in his attitude towards the midwives.

'Toby's amazing when it comes to liaising with us over patients and being at the birth or not, according to what people want,' said Melanie. 'I'm sure he'll make a super father,' she added sincerely.

'I think so too,' Rachel agreed, 'but we were talking about you.'

'I know it's boring in comparison with your news,' said Melanie,' but I'm really happy at work. These six or seven months with Bridget have been the happiest of my life, Rachel. I honestly don't feel any need to retire.'

They paid their bill, Rachel having just given her

friend a warm look in reply to this last comment. They stepped out into the busy little street together.

'No telling, please, Melanie. Jackie'll be furious, but not half so mad as Toby'll be if he finds out I've been letting the cat out of the bag at this stage.'

Rachel's sister, Jackie, was a real rural earth mother. She lived in a terraced cottage on the outskirts of Brighton's busy centre, made her own everything from marmalade to dresses, and had two children under three on whose behalf she was tireless. She produced potato-cut pictures and plasticine masterpieces between making the beds and cooking Cordon Bleu meals for all and sundry, and never seemed to stop talking. The only thing in the home that escaped her care and attention was the housework which accumulated gradually and relentlessly until it ceased to pose any threat to order and became the environment itself.

Once this happened, as Rachel had long ago pointed out to Melanie, it became completely unnecessary to do any. The dirt merged into the general background and everybody developed antibodies to it.

Melanie loved staying at Jackie's. She was a superb cook and her husband, who nursed at a local hospital for mentally handicapped children, regularly brought people home to eat and sleep. The festive atmosphere that resulted from this 'open house' was enchanting. There always seemed to be enough to eat, enough home-made wine to drink and interesting talk around the table.

Jackie loved company and would unroll unending numbers of sleeping bags at the end of the evening. She had never settled into a career herself and was blissfully happy having babies and looking after John, her husband. As soon as he got an annual salary increment, she would be pregnant again, with his full approval. And if they had to sell the car to make ends meet, then so be it.

Their life fascinated Melanie. She was shocked by the disorder, but warmed through and through by the welcome, and by the time a day had flown by she always

wished time would stop instead. She listened to John
talking about his beloved handicapped children and
learned from him, then she went into the kitchen and
learned about cooking from Jackie. Their home was a
real home to her, who could hardly recall her own.

The promenade was calm and peaceful as Rachel and
Melanie made their way to Jackie's. Some brave holi-
daymakers were huddling behind windscreens on the
beach, but most had decided to enjoy the breezy afternoon as the two girls had done, in the shops and outside
cafés.

'England!' muttered Rachel.

'We'd be invaded with tourists if the weather was
warmer,' said Melanie philosophically.

Much later, Melanie walked along the same stretch by
herself. The news of Rachel's engagement, happy as she
was for her friend, had stirred up all sorts of feeling
inside her and she had been pleased for the excuse to go
out alone when the grandparents had turned up this
evening. As she walked the evening breeze tugged at her
light coat and blew the hair back from her face. She
thrust her hands deep into her coat pockets and set her
face against the wind.

All along the promenade couples strolled, hand in
hand or huddled together, arms around one another. If
anything, there were more people around this evening
than there had been this afternoon. But all couples, it
seemed. Grey and pink clouds lingered in the western
sky, and as she watched they darkened and disappeared
into the indigo night.

She turned down towards the sea and leaned against
the rail that topped the sea wall. Lights danced out along
the length of the old pier, and far out to sea she could
discern the lights of a passenger vessel heading out
majestically.

The whole wide world is out there, Melanie thought.
The idea had a calming effect after the couples behind
her, each of whom seemed to reinforce the impression

that everyone had a mate but her. The whole wide world. And I can do anything, she thought. My world doesn't stop at the practice, or even here, at the southern edge of England.

Her mind drifted back to the conversation she had had with Rachel. A pretty house with a garden, a husband and a child. Was this what she wanted too? She pushed away a strand of dark hair which the wind had blown across her eyes and stared after the ship on the horizon. No, she was not at all sure that she wanted to settle down in a pretty house with a garden. The thought of gardens and greenery catapulted her back on to a spring hillside with Daniel Davenport.

'This is what I miss . . .' he had said. What would I miss? Melanie tried to think for the first time in her life of what she really wanted from it. To her surprise, she decided firmly against a house and garden. It would be nice to travel, she thought. The ship had almost disappeared. She screwed up her eyes and could just make it out still, steaming slowly away.

Yes, it would be nice to travel. She faced the fact in her imagination: that she would like not to travel alone. She would like not to be always alone. And she would like to work. She would like always to be able to be a midwife.

Was it too much to ask to have both? However hard she tried not to, she had now to think of Dr Davenport and his different destiny. He too was committed to his career. If what Rachel had said was true and he was indeed to have the Chair in Obstetrics at the SWCH, how would he go forward? Into national popular fame, like Prof. Young? No, Melanie did not think so. She imagined him choosing a much more introverted academic path: international lecture tours, research, clinical teaching, perhaps an overseas appointment . . .

Melanie bit her lip. And she? After a couple of years she would begin to think about starting up her own practice. Already the case-load at their practice was too much for her and Bridget. Gradually, they both hoped,

public demand for their service would be such that many
new independent midwives would be tempted into their
field.

Demand would grow, and gradually their own profession would begin to recover control over midwifery,
and medicine would begin to stand aside and allow the
old relationship of trust to emerge again between
women and their midwives. Slowly, things would
change.

Did she have the stamina to devote her life to this end?
Melanie's eyes smarted. She blinked and resumed her
vigil. Across the empty darkened beach waves crept forward, silently lapped the black sand and then retreated.

It was not only their careers that would keep herself
and Daniel Davenport apart, she considered, her mind
stubbornly returning to the old subject once more.
There was the past—whatever had happened to put
those sleepless shadows beneath his eyes and to turn his
young manhood suddenly and irretrievably into granite
maturity.

There was all that. And then there was the woman.
Buying the black dress had reminded her of that perfect
creature at the Ball. How lovely she had been, smiling at
him across the table, apparently unperturbed by his
dancing with someone else. But of course she, Melanie,
posed no real threat to such a woman; she was no rival,
not even in the same race. Such a woman could afford to
humour his whims where other women were concerned.
Melanie recalled his kiss, the humour in his eyes. Yes,
she was certainly a whim.

Melanie blamed the now bitter wind for the tears that
had sprung to her eyes. She forced her hands away from
the railing and found them stiff with cold. She pulled her
coat around her and turned back to the promenade.

The pubs were full of smoke and laughter and the
theatres quiet, in mid-programme. The hotel res-
taurants were busy with late pairs of diners. Melanie
walked slowly back to her adopted home. In some ways,
she reflected, she would be glad to get back to work.

'Bye, Mella, see you next year, if not before!' Jackie waved from the doorway, a baby on each hip.

Rachel flashed Melanie a guilty look. She still had not told her sister about Toby—or at least, not that she was going to marry him at Christmas.

'I'll be in touch soon,' she called.

''Bye. Thanks for everything again,' waved Melanie. The gate clicked closed behind them. 'I don't know how you did it,' she said to Rachel the minute they were out of earshot, 'she's as guileless as a child.'

'That's how I did it,' Rachel admitted. 'It's easy not to tell a child something that has to be shared with a grown-up first. As soon as I've met the Majors, I'll bring Toby down to meet my folks and Jackie. It'll be love at first sight between them all, of course. It's Toby's parents who need coaxing—their only son, etc., etc.'

'Still, I don't know how you kept quiet.'

'Nor do I. Telling you helped, just as I was bursting to tell someone.'

They bought tickets for a Victoria-bound train. Ten minutes later they were watching the Sussex Downs spreading away on either side and out of their reach as they sped towards London. Usually Melanie experienced pangs of regret as Haywards Heath heralded the end of the countryside and the beginning of the urban area, but today she was almost pleased to be heading in this direction.

Glancing at Rachel opposite, she saw that she felt similarly. But it was not work that beckoned Rachel back to London so seductively. For a long time, almost into the grimy outskirts of the city, Melanie pondered the revolution in one's life that resulted from falling in love. How all the plans one had made got changed and all the previous loyalties and priorities rearranged!

But by eight o'clock the following morning, all such ruminations were far behind her. Bridget had time to spend just an hour with her, bringing her up to date with all that had happened in her absence before she herself had to leave for the start of her RCM refresher course.

'I did the home visit to Julia Young last week and she's due another tomorrow. She was fine. Gained a kilo in weight and her BP is steady at 130/70 . . .'

'Oh, it's down. Thank goodness!' interposed Melanie.

'She's looking forward to seeing you. All other obs were normal, urine, NAD, etc. The baby sounds fine. I was impressed by the home environment, of course. Not too many contra-indications for a home confinement there!'

'I haven't really seen the whole house yet, just the areas we usually check. I'm hoping for a guided tour tomorrow.'

'Well, I once delivered a beautiful nine-pound boy on a heap of dirty newspapers on the bedroom floor because Granny was in the only bed. The three other children were all agog at the proceedings; they'd never seen hot water before except in the teapot. And the toilet was out in the yard.'

Melanie grinned. 'Yes, I don't think the Young delivery will be quite that primitive.'

'The stupid thing is, it doesn't seem to make much difference,' commented Bridget philosophically. 'I found sugar in her urine one ante-natal visit, then realised she'd just given me a sample out of a swilled-out jampot! Afterwards she put the jam back. Nobody seemed any the worse for it. All the kids were thriving —so much for keeping ourselves up to date with sterile procedures and high-tech delivery! See you! I'm taking my bleep. But don't hesitate to call me away if you need me. Please!' Bridget winked, waved and was gone.

Melanie ran her eye down the long list of notes she had made. At the top she had written: 'Amina—collect babe, check post-natal care with DD.' Amina's baby would be two weeks old tomorrow and Melanie had promised she would accompany her ex-client to the hospital to bring him home.

It was a nice job for a Monday morning, especially the first morning back at work after the holiday. Melanie welcomed the locum midwife, Jenny Stiles, whose help she and Bridget had enlisted often before. Jenny was officially 'retired', but she filled in for them when one or another was away and was an invaluable third pair of hands at short notice on the rare occasions when two deliveries happened simultaneously.

'We shouldn't be busy this morning, Jenny, what with holidays and the "silly season" starting. There are only seven down for ante-natal this morning. But I should be back by midday.'

'Don't rush,' said Jenny, 'I'm in the mood for work. I got my hand back in properly while you were on holiday.'

'Yes, you've been pretty busy,' said Melanie.

'Frantic! Loved every minute of it.'

'You should come back full-time,' said Melanie, 'start up a new practice.'

'Funny you should say that—it's been crossing and re-crossing my mind,' said Jenny.

Melanie grabbed her bag and glanced at herself in the small mirror in the hall. She looked presentable in her soft blue dress. It felt good to be back at work.

She drove to Amina's house and parked outside. At the front door she was met by an immaculately dressed Amina. In the background hovered the mother-in-law. It was the first time that Melanie had noticed how tall and imposing the older woman was in contrast to her fragile daughter-in-law.

But nothing could dampen Amina's spirits today.

'I am so glad to see you again,' she said, her eyes shining. 'How was your holiday?'

Melanie walked to the car beside her tiny companion in her golden-threaded sari. 'Lovely, thank you, Amina. How have you been?'

'Also well. I have come out of the hospital one week ago. Only now I am longing to have my baby home.'

They drove to Lessing Lane in silence, and Melanie parked at the front so that they would not have far to walk.

The staff in the nursery next to the Special Care Baby

Unit were obviously sad to let little Baby Chowdhary go. One of the pupil midwives was wrapping him gently in a white lacy shawl and another was cooing farewell to him while she did so.

'If you manage to get hold of him, Amina,' smiled Melanie, 'I'll just find Sister. She's sure to want to give you your post-natal appointment and an update on Saleem.'

She left mother and baby, both looking very pleased with themselves, and went in search of Sister—never an easy job in the SCBU or the Nursery, where everyone wore the same blue dresses and covered their hair with the same paper caps. Sister was not to be seen in the Nursery or the station, but in the incubator room a masked figure approached Melanie. She recognised Rachel.

'Hi, Mella! I didn't expect to see you again so soon!'

Rachel pulled down her mask.

'I've come to collect Baby Chowdhary. He was the Caesar just before our holiday, remember? But I'd clean forgotten to tell you I'd be in today for him. Where's Sister?'

'Here. Or rather, I'm Acting Sister. Judith's rushed off on one of those RCM refresher courses . . .'

'Bridget too!' rejoined Melanie. 'Well, we obviously didn't spend the whole holiday talking shop. Have you got time to discharge little Saleem now?'

'Hold on a tick . . .' Rachel poked her head back inside the incubator room and said something to one of her staff. 'Right!'

In Sister's office, Amina looked obediently at the report and appointment cards for herself and Saleem. It was perfectly plain that she was taking in nothing of what was said to her. Melanie knew this would happen; little or no medical information past the fact that the baby was thriving would penetrate Amina's excitement today. That was why she was here.

'And so you'll come back to the hospital for your six-week post-natal check-up on the twentieth,' Rachel

reiterated patiently, 'and bring Saleem in to be seen by
the paediatrician the same morning.'

Amina looked puzzled.

'But I thought Melanie would see me at home for this
examination?' she said, cradling her child protectively in
her arms. 'I did not think I would have to come back to
the hospital.'

'Your son must be checked by the hospital children's
doctor, Mrs Chowdhary,' came an authoritative voice
—a masculine voice.

Daniel Davenport had entered the room unseen and
pulled the door quietly to behind him. Rachel, Amina
and Melanie were clustered around Sister's desk, and
Melanie's back was to the door. She spun round at the
sound of his voice, and the colour flew to her face.

'We were just explaining that to Mrs Chowdhary,' she
flared.

The consultant regarded her levelly, then ran his
fingers through his thick fair hair. Rachel shot Melanie a
glance, then looked back to Dr Davenport, then back to
her flatmate again. It was plain from her eyes what she
had seen.

'Mrs Chowdhary quite understands about her
appointments, Dr Davenport, and we can answer her
questions, thank you,' Rachel stated quietly.

'I shall come to the hospital,' said Amina.

'Of course, if Miss Aarts wishes to follow up her client
herself, that's quite acceptable,' the consultant continued as if neither of the two women had spoken. 'Just
so long as we see this little fellow again to check up on
him.'

He chucked the baby delicately under the chin, and
Baby Chowdhary opened his eyes and regarded him
seriously.

'Well, will you visit Mrs Chowdhary yourself, Miss
Aarts?' he asked.

'Er—yes.'

'Fine. Then you must bring little—what's his name?'
he turned to Amina.

'Saleem,' whispered Amina.

'Ah, yes. Bring Saleem in to see the children's doctor
in six weeks, and Miss Aarts will see you at home. I'm
sure she can manage that. Now, what have you got for
me today, Staff Lewis?'

He turned his attention to Rachel, who lifted her
eyebrows at Melanie and concealed a smile, composing
her features into an expression befitting a unit round
with a senior member of the medical staff.

'I'll be with you now, Dr Davenport,' she said. 'Goodbye, Saleem. Goodbye and good luck, Mrs Chowdhary.
I'll see you tonight, Mella,' she muttered as she held the
door open for the consultant and then for Amina.

Not for the first time lately, Melanie was grateful to
see the back of Lessing Lane. And not for the first time,
she wished Rachel was a little less quick to jump to
conclusions.

She parked outside the Chowdhary home and opened
the car back door for Amina. Amina stepped out and
across the pavement like a queen, her diminutive stature
not detracting from the regal impression in the least. Her
son looked up at her with enormous dark-fringed eyes.
Amina proudly met her mother-in-law, who had just
opened the front door, and for the first time, Melanie
saw the older woman's features soften in a smile.

'Welcome,' she said, in her unpractised English,' my
child. My children, welcome home!'

If Melanie had been mildly annoyed by Dr Davenport's
somewhat patronising attitude towards her over
Amina's post-natal care, she was positively infuriated by
her own response to him. She fumed at herself during
the drive back to the practice, and she continued to
simmer while she worked methodically through the
cases that arrived for the afternoon ante-natal clinic.

It wouldn't have been so bad had Rachel not been
there. But Rachel had been very much there, and much
as Melanie loved Rachel, her tongue-wagging was a little
hard to take sometimes. All that Melanie could do was

to hope that this would be confined to an audience of one at Bedford Park. But she knew it was a vain hope.

If Rachel resisted the temptation to share her supposition about Melanie and Dr Davenport with a few close friends at Lessing Lane—which Melanie doubted—she would certainly not balk at sharing it with Toby. Melanie shivered at the thought.

It had only been a blush, a momentary loss of poise, but that was more than enough to set the grapevine at Lessing Lane humming. She hoped that the consultant's offhand manner with her had been enough to dampen the effect upon Rachel of that first contact.

She screwed the disposable sheeting that she had just pulled off the couch into a ball and threw it violently towards the wastepaper bin. It missed. She picked it up and tugged at the roll to replace it, before realising that she had just seen her last client. She calmed herself by tidying up thoroughly and carefully, then made herself a cup of coffee.

She wished Bridget was there, or Jenny, but Jenny had left half an hour before. Sipping her coffee, she decided to go to a film tonight. Anything would be better than sitting alone in the flat waiting for the phone to ring and summon her to a delivery, her mind going round and round in circles. And then when Rachel got in, the inquisition. If she went to a film she would be able to laugh the whole thing off by the time she saw her flatmate again.

She got up and rang the telephone paging service who contacted her when Bridget was away and she was already busy. She left details with them, saying she would ring them with the number of the cinema, just to be sure, and asking them to check her bleep. This done, she washed up her coffee cup. Enough was enough, she decided, for the first day back at work after her holiday.

She reached the front door just as the bell went. Opening it, she stared dumbfounded at the tall figure who confronted her, and took an involuntary step backwards. He came indoors.

'Just in time to catch you, I see, Miss Aarts. May I come in?'

Melanie acknowledged the formality and closed the door behind him. She followed Dr Davenport down the corridor and back into the room which she had just left. Suddenly, instead of feeling cool and airy as it had done a few moments ago, the room seemed stuffy, oppressive and hot. Melanie recognised the latter, at least, as self-generated.

'What can I do for you?' she asked.

Dr Davenport gave her an appraising look. He had put a blue folder of Lessing Lane case notes down on the table and was now standing calmly by the French windows. Drawing aside the gauze curtain, he looked at the little patch of garden. Bridget had planted it with wall-flowers, pansies and geraniums, all of which were in full flower.

'Very nice—very nice indeed. Quite a pleasant little set-up you've got here.'

'I'm glad you like it,' Melanie heard herself say. Exasperated, she wondered if she would ever be able to frame an intelligent remark in the presence of this man. 'You're very welcome to look round,' she invited, 'although there's very little high technology to interest you here.'

'What makes you think I'm particularly interested in advanced technology, Melanie?'

Melanie jumped. He had done this to her so often before: just as she got used to a certain mode of communication, a certain professional distance, he would suddenly use her first name . . .

'I don't know, really . . .' she said.

'No, you don't really know, do you, Melanie?' His voice was quiet, almost soft. 'It's a great mistake to make assumptions, Melanie, especially negative assumptions about another person. You suppose that you, perhaps, are the only radical thinker in obstetrics, that you . . .'

'I think nothing of the sort,' interrupted Melanie, confused, 'I . . .'

'Please don't interrupt me. I said "perhaps". But there are those, Melanie, who are neither extremely radical nor reactionary. Those whose views had been modified and moulded by their experience—perhaps quite broad experience. Such people are not boring middle-of-the-roaders, Melanie, but thinking, feeling, *responsible* practitioners and people.'

The stress on the word 'responsible' was unmistakable. Melanie tried to absorb his words without over-reacting to them, but she felt her reaction boiling up inside her.

'Such people do not judge others, perhaps as harshly, as hastily . . .' he paused significantly, '. . . but now I'm riding a hobbyhorse of my own. And perhaps you don't consider this a fit occasion, so I'll stop.'

Melanie stared at the man opposite her as though he had just stepped off Mars. Her mind was teeming, but somehow no words presented themselves to her but two completely inappropriate ones: 'persecution' and 'complex'.

'Would you like some coffee?' she faltered.

'No, thank you. I'm on my way home. I thought you'd need Mrs Chowdhary's medical notes to complement the ward reports on her and her baby. Please be sure to return them promptly when you've discharged your client.'

He patted the blue folder on his way out of the room. Melanie followed him meekly to the front door. There he lifted one finger to indicate that she need not come farther, just as he had done on numerous occasions during ward rounds. He neither said goodbye, nor smiled, but behaved as though his mind was already somewhere else.

Melanie leaned against the back of the front door and let out her breath. So he called in to lecture me, and now he's on his way home, she thought. She tried to remember what her plan had been for this evening. 'I'm on my way home . . .' Oh, God! she thought.

CHAPTER NINE

JULIA was looking magnificent, her brown arms and legs bearing witness to afternoon rests taken in the sun. She was wearing a white maternity dress which accentuated the effect of her fair hair and tan.

'You look terrific!' Melanie exclaimed.

'You too. Come round to the back and have some lemon tea—it's just made.'

Julia led her round the side of the huge house and they emerged into a garden where white chairs and a table were grouped beneath the trees. It was a haven of tranquillity; a walled garden where the sound of traffic did not penetrate.

Melanie sat down and accepted a cup of fragrant tea. The smell of lemon mingled with that of the flowers in the nearby border. Butterflies danced above the up-turned flower heads and birds sang in the trees. Julia looked sheepishly at Melanie.

'Aren't I lazy? I sit all day while you're working away in a stuffy old practice! I read the occasional magazine and make the odd cup of tea, and barely stir myself to get a salad on the table for poor Malcolm when he comes home from the hospital. And hardly a pang of what you'd call real conscience. Disgusting, isn't it?'

'Oh, I don't know,' reflected Melanie. 'I could force myself into that frame of mind, I think. I could develop a taste for a couple of weeks of it. How are you feeling?' She sipped her tea. 'Any signs of imminent arrival?'

'Not a sausage!'

'September the tenth, isn't it?' We're nearly there.'

'I don't feel as if it's going to make an appearance next week,' Julia admitted, 'but then, never having done this before, I could be wrong.'

'Anyway, I'm delighted to hear your BP's stayed down.'

They drank their tea and Melanie told Julia about Brighton and generally gossiped about her holiday.

'Well, I suppose you want to examine us,' said Julia at last. 'And I promised to show you around the house too. We'll work our way through from back to front, then go upstairs.'

She led Melanie through the conservatory towards the back door of the house. The warmth in the glass room was almost stifling. A vine had thrown its emerald trailers all across the ceiling, from which hung heavy clusters of half-ripe fruit. A peach tree stood beside the door, carrying three perfect peaches.

'How lovely, to grow grapes and peaches!' exclaimed Melanie.

'That's Malcolm,' said Julia. 'He's got green fingers.'

They went on into the house, which was fresh and cool after the conservatory. It was an old building, thick-walled with high moulded ceilings and spacious public rooms. Each had a large marble fireplace and big windows. Everything was so calm that Melanie had difficulty imagining how a child was going to fit in to such dignified surroundings.

'Oh, and you didn't see the nursery,' Julia said in answer to her thoughts. 'We hadn't done it up when you were last here, had we?'

'No. I'd love to see it.'

'Well, we'll start here. This is the downstairs study. It used to be the drawing room, but now we hardly ever use it. I come in here sometimes to read, and Malcolm to work if I'm watching television in the other room . . .'

But Melanie had stopped hearing Julia. She was transfixed by a photograph in an old ebony frame which sat upon the antique bureau. It was quite a recent and recognisable photograph of the woman who had been with Daniel Davenport at the May Ball.

'What are you looking at?' asked Julia, coming and standing behind her. 'Oh, Miranda! Gorgeous, isn't she? It's not fair. I'm not only the elder, but also the ugly sister!'

Sisters! That was it. Melanie looked at the portrait and then at Julia and wondered how she had missed the likeness before. It was true that Julia was less delicate than her sister in appearance, but the family resemblance was nevertheless very strong. Even the contrast between the fair Julia and Miranda's dark beauty did not detract from it.

'She is beautiful,' murmured Melanie, her mind filling with questions which could not be asked.

'Beautiful. And clever too—she's a surgeon,' explained Julia. 'I tell you, it's not fair. If we weren't so close I'd be positively jealous!' She laughed and led Melanie out of the room, closing the door softly behind them.

She conducted Melanie round other rooms, but Melanie hardly saw them. She was totally occupied with Miranda and Daniel Davenport. It all made sense to her now: the family intimacy between him and Julia that allowed her such familiarity with him. He was married to her sister. What a perfectly matched pair they were, and how stupid of her not to have seen the likeness between the two women and put two and two together before now. She could have saved herself so much pain and uncertainty.

And obviously the obstetrician was concerned for Julia's health and safety—his own family! She had been not only stupid, but blind and self-centred enough to connect his concern with her. Recently, she had even allowed herself to dream that he too was anxious that this supreme test of her midwifery skills should go well. What a fool she had been!

She followed Julia up the broad staircase, haunted by the serene smile in the ebony frame.

'. . . and this is the nursery.'

Julia threw open a door and the smell of freshly-laundered linen met them. Inside, the room was a pool of sunlight. A frieze of yellow marching ducks paraded around the walls, and the cot and chest of drawers had been painted to match. On a shelf above the changing mat stood a buttercup-coloured hairbrush and talcum powder container, and beside them a brand new teddy bear. Propped beside him sat the little silver Victorian teething ring.

Melanie swallowed the lump that had risen to her throat.

'It's beautiful, Julia,' she said. 'What a lovely room!'

Next door, in the big blue-and-white-decorated master bedroom, Melanie examined her client. Everything was exactly as it should be. While she was listening to the foetal heart, Julia had a Braxton Hicks contraction.

'They've been coming and going for a couple of weeks as strong as that,' commented Julia. 'But they never seem to get any stronger.'

'Well, call me the minute they do, Julia,' said Melanie. 'Don't go leaving it for ages before you do, will you?'

Julia shook her head, smiling.

'Promise?'

'I do believe you're as worried as I am about this babe, Melanie. Your eyes just gave you away.'

'I've admitted it before now,' returned Melanie. 'I just don't want to miss all the fun and get here to find the Prof.'s delivered the baby while I popped out for a quick cuppa—that's happened before now!' she grinned.

'Don't you worry—not this one. I want you to deliver me as much as you do, Malcolm or no Malcolm. Sometimes one wants a woman around as well as a special husband. I feel very lucky to have both,' said Julia.

A sultry September the tenth came and went and still there was no sign of Julia's baby. Melanie counted the days, jumped each time the phone rang and started having trouble sleeping. She hadn't been called out to a night time delivery for ages. The long sleepy summer days seemed to have lulled Nature herself to sleep.

Rachel was blissfully happy, now openly planning her Christmas wedding. The interview with Toby's parents had gone well, in spite of her nervous preparations, and they had been delighted that Toby was going to settle down at last with 'a medical lass'. As for Rachel's own family, they had reacted just as she had predicted that they would.

Gradually and vaguely, Melanie's anxiety that Julia Young should deliver soon had become confused with a much more personal matter. She had begun to realise that until Julia's confinement was over, her links with Lessing Lane—or more specifically with a senior member of the medical staff there—could not be severed.

She called on Julia again for a weekly ante-natal visit, and once more they drank tea together on the lawn. Again, all was well both with her and with the unborn child. There were still no signs of an impending delivery, and Julia was her usual calm, amused and philosophical self.

'Of course,' she remarked, 'Malcolm's been pestering me about an induction. In the nicest possible way, you understand.' Her eyes twinkled in the sunlight.

Melanie wanted for her to go on, but she didn't.

'How do you feel about that?' Melanie asked at last.

Julia smiled as serenely as the sister in the photograph. 'I feel it's completely unnecessary,' she stated. 'Even *I* remember that first babies are often late.'

'I was going to mention induction as a possibility if nothing had happened by today,' said Melanie.

'Yes, I thought you might,' Julia returned, 'but I think we should let Nature take her course, don't you? More tea?'

'Thank you, yes. It's delicious,' said Melanie. 'I agree with you. It wasn't Nature who decided that every pregnancy should last exactly two hundred and eighty days, after all. That isn't how she works at all.'

'Exactly,' replied Julia, 'what I told Malcolm last night.' She smiled the same sweet smile which Melanie felt sure that she had employed last night too.

Melanie drove back to the practice through streets whose dusty lethargy bore testimony to the long hot summer. Even in her light cotton dress she felt stifled, and the open car windows admitted air as thick and warm as soup.

She pushed open the front door into the cool practice and heard the sounds of Jenny's and Bridget's voices with pleasure. The clinic must be quiet this afternoon. She sat down with the other two and began to unwind.

'How's Julia?' asked Bridget, pouring Melanie a glass of orange juice.

'Fine. But nothing's happening.'

'She must be overdue?'

'Only a couple of days. She's not worried about it. The Professor has suggested to her that she has an induction, but she wants to let things go on naturally.'

'That reminds me . . .' Bridget stood up and found a letter on her desk. 'This came for you by special messenger from Lessing Lane.'

Melanie took the letter and tore it open. She read:

'Dear Miss Aarts,

re Amina Chowdhary

Due to the increasing risks of placenta praevia occurring in subsequent pregnancies, the above patient should be advised that future deliveries will also be managed by late hospitalisation and Caesarean section. No other special advice need be given at routine post-natal visit.

Thanks for seeing this patient.

D. Davenport.'

'Cheek!' muttered Melanie under her breath. When she finally looked up, both Bridget and Jenny were looking expectantly at her.

'Well?' queried Jenny.

'Is the School of Midwifery offering you a visiting lectureship?' asked Bridget. 'You look slightly bemused.'

It wasn't that unusual to get notes from Lessing Lane

when there was liaison between a midwife and a hospital consultant over a case, and Melanie realised that her colour had given her away yet again.

'Not exactly,' she blushed still. 'It's one of the consultants explaining to me how a placenta praevia bodes ill for future pregnancies and spontaneous deliveries. He says to be sure to tell Amina that she'll be having Caesars from now on. As if I didn't already know!' she finished with irritation.

'Not your famous Dr Davenport?' asked Bridget lightly. She added for Jenny's benefit, 'Melanie has a love-hate relationship with the most attractive of her ex-chiefs at Lessing Lane. They're like oil and water.'

'Oh, yes?' Jenny lifted her eyebrows and her glass simultaneously, and sighed with mock resignation. 'Well, you know what I've always thought about these recurrent tiffs. The course of true love, etc. Anyway,' she winked at Bridget, 'I must be off.'

Bridget too, it seemed, was amused. 'If you're passing Lessing Lane, Jen, you might take an answer in for the doctor. I'm sure you could scribble a note in a moment, just to say Get lost, I know my own job—couldn't you, Melanie?'

Melanie felt herself getting flustered again.

'What more can you expect from snooty obstetricians?' she tried to sound unconcerned. It was hard to tell whether her colleagues were taken in, but somehow she did not think so.

A little while later, she threw her bag once more into the back seat of her car, opened all the windows, and drove home. Whether it was the heat, anxiety over Julia or annoyance over the communication that she had just had, she didn't know, but she was as irritable as a fevered child.

Her anger was made worse by the thought that Rachel would be around when she got back to the flat and would probably be keen to show her yet another dress bought in the summer sales on her day off, in preparation for her honeymoon. The very thought of weddings was enough to increase the temperature inside the car by ten degrees!

She cooled down over the next few days, in spite of increasing fears that Julia would end up in hospital with a Syntocinon drip in her arm. They can't induce her against her will, she kept telling herself. Yet with a husband as concerned and influential as Malcolm Young, with family as medical and anti-midwifery as Daniel Davenport . . .

Melanie held the same internal dialogue with herself a thousand times. And then, on a Monday evening just two days short of forty-one weeks, Julia rang to say that she was in labour.

'They're not too bad, about every twenty minutes,' she said. 'And Malcolm's here and I'm fine. This is just an early warning!' she laughed.

As usual, Melanie was amazed at Julia's air of self-sufficiency. But most of all, she felt a great wave of relief that her labour had begun spontaneously and that, so far, all was going well.

Melanie went to bed but could not sleep. It was the early hours of the morning before she did so, and then she awoke with a start to find that it was eight a.m. —nine hours since Julia had rung. Melanie's heart was racing as she thought of Julia's age and how she might be so far into a long and difficult labour. She calmed herself, deciding to call in at Julia's on her way into the practice. If anything was wrong, she would have been notified.

'Hello, Melanie. How are you?'

Prof. Young smiled genially and welcomed his ex-staff midwife into his home as if she was a regular visitor —which she supposed she now was. Still, it was very strange to see him there. This was the first time that she had actually seen the Professor since leaving Lessing Lane. He had put her at ease by addressing her by her first name, as if he fully shared his wife's trust in her chosen professional helper and respected her choice.

'Hello, Prof. Young,' returned Melanie. 'How are things with your wife?'

'Slow, but fine, I think. But what am I thinking about, keeping you standing here? Come in, m'dear.'

Melanie followed the neat familiar figure of the Professor upstairs. He was just as he was at Lessing Lane: dapper, sweet and in control.

Julia smiled a slightly weaker than usual smile as Melanie entered her bedroom. 'Oh, good, Melanie. I was just on the point of asking Malcolm to ring you. I think the waters broke about two, didn't they, Malcolm?'

'Two-ten, to be exact,' affirmed the Professor. 'I'll leave you to your client, Melanie.' He discreetly closed the door behind him.

'He seems to be enjoying himself, anyway,' said Julia with one of her old wry looks. 'Actually, he's been super,' she added sincerely.

Melanie measured Julia's blood pressure and pulse and found them to be satisfactory. The foetal heartbeat was strong and regular and internal examination revealed the cervix to be two centimetres dilated. The baby was lying normally ready for a vertex delivery.

All this information was relayed to Julia. She closed her eyes in disappointment when she heard how far she had progressed.

'I thought I must be much further on than that,' she sighed. 'Melanie, do you have to go? Or can you stay?'

It was obviously going to be a long slow process until the baby came. Melanie tried to remember how many clients were down for the clinic this morning, but she couldn't.

'I'll phone my partner,' she said, 'I'll be back in a minute, Julia.'

'Stay where you are, Melanie,' said Bridget without hesitation. 'I don't need you here, so just concentrate on the job in hand and don't worry about anything else. And Melanie?'

'Yes?'

'Good luck!'

'Thanks, Bridget,' replied Melanie, so relieved she could hardly thank her.

Julia's delight was in her eyes when Melanie told her that she could stay from now on.

'Would you like to get up for a while and wander around? It might take your mind off things a bit,' she suggested.

'I'd love to. Malcolm said to stay in bed until you'd come and checked up on me,' said Julia, 'but if you say so . . .'

Melanie helped Julia to get up and wash, put her hair up and dress in a clean nightdress. After helping her client downstairs, she made up the bed freshly with protective sheeting and laid out her things in preparation for the birth.

Only when she was satisfied that everything was ready did she follow Julia downstairs. Prof. Young had done all he could to put her at her ease, and yet the unfamiliar situation now that he was there too made Melanie very nervous.

Julia matter-of-factly carried out the instructions of her National Childbirth Trust instructor as the contractions came and went, and Melanie and the Professor were left with nothing to do but exchange conversation.

'Marvellous chap, Grantly Dick-Reed,' he observed, 'brilliant to put together such a simple sum: fear equals tension equals pain. Of course, some daft idiot immediately misheard him and said natural childbirth meant painless childbirth and gave the whole thing a bad name. Typical doctor, eh, Melanie?'

His wife gasped softly and then relaxed.

'But education and information do help to break the vicious circle, removing the fear produced by ignorance. Isn't that so, Julia?' He looked fondly and mischievously at his wife.

'Tell him you're not in the School now, for God's sake, Melanie,' said Julia.

Melanie looked affectionately at Professor Young. She recognised in him excitement which could express itself only in streams of words.

'I will when I get bored,' she promised Julia.

'Coffee?' offered the Professor. 'Tea? Orange juice?'

'Nothing, thank you very much,' replied Melanie. 'I think it's time I had another look at your wife.'

It was almost midday when the doorbell rang and Melanie heard Toby Robertson's voice downstairs. Julia was resting as best she could between contractions which were coming every five minutes, but the cervix was still only three centimetres dilated.

When Melanie came down to the cool airy living room, Toby and Professor Young were deep in conversation at the other end of it. The Professor looked up as Melanie entered.

'How are things going?' he asked.

She told him.

'Dr Robertson and myself have been having a word or two. What do you think about speeding things up a bit? Perhaps a spot of Valium or something? She's getting tired.'

Melanie nodded.

'I've just come down to say that Julia and I were just talking about that. But she doesn't want anything. She says she'll be fine and doesn't want to be doped. I've explained what we'd give her, but she's adamant.'

Toby and the Professor gave one another a shrug, and the Professor said he'd be up in a minute, as Melanie dashed from the room and back upstairs. She was full of admiration for him, being able to stand aside and allow her to care for his wife like this. For the first time she realised what a difficult position, potentially, Julia had put him into by coming to see her at the beginning of her pregnancy. Even given that Julia had had no way of knowing that Melanie was a newly-resigned member of his own midwifery team.

He must love his wife very much indeed, Melanie decided. And Julia deserved his love and respect. She was working very hard. Never had Melanie understood so fully how aptly named was labour. She opened the bedroom windows wide and let in the fragrant flower-scented air. Hardly a breath of wind stirred in the garden below. The white table and chairs stood vacant on the grass, as if awaiting Julia.

At last, at about four, the day began to cool. Melanie examined Julia again and this time she knew that the birth was very near. Julia, still in full control of her own body and labour, had refused repeated offers of seda-tives, painkillers and Entonox.

She went into second stage almost without a murmur, responding obediently to Melanie's guidance, so that her urge to push was used to best effect.

Melanie hardly noticed Professor Young and Toby come to the bedroom. The Professor smoothed his wife's forehead and sat down in the chair that Melanie had placed close to the head of the bed. He held Julia's hand and whispered encouragement to her. Toby had rolled up his sleeves and stood near Melanie, waiting for instructions which never came. The rhythm of the birth process was so well established by now that Julia and her midwife seemed to be part of the same machine. It was impossible to tell which was initiating and which responding to the actions as the birth proceeded.

Melanie laid the palm of her right hand over the top of the baby's head while it emerged, then rotated through ninety degrees to face the inside of its mother's left thigh. Another push, and one shoulder was born. Melanie administered ergometrine into Julia's hip, to contract down the uterus after the baby's birth and help separation and delivery of the afterbirth.

The second shoulder, and then the rest of a little baby girl slid into Melanie's waiting hands. She wiped the eyes, nose and mouth and sucked out a little fluid. The baby let out a yell.

'She's perfect!' said Melanie.

Julia opened her eyes and looked at her daughter. Then she turned to her husband. He, with tears in his

eyes, bent and kissed her swiftly on the lips, while
Melanie looked away.

The baby lay quietly on Julia's abdomen while Melanie tied and cut the cord. At last Professor Young said,

'I bet you never expected to hear my wife lost for
words, did you, Melanie?'

Melanie could only smile.

'She's lovely,' she said. And suddenly everyone was
either laughing, or crying, or both at once.

When they were alone together, the delivery was completed and Julia washed and settled in a fresh bed. The
baby was also bathed and dressed and laid in her cot next
to Julia's bed, where she had fallen peacefully asleep.

Melanie looked into the cot.

'She's really beautiful, Julia. She really is.'

'Do you know what we're going to call her?'

'What?'

'Melanie, after you,' said Julia simply. 'And Miranda
after my sister. Melanie Miranda Young. What do you
think?'

Melanie looked up from packing away her equipment
and documentation. Her heart was beating painfully.

'Oh, Julia,' she smiled, 'that's a real honour!'

'And we'd like you both to be godmothers too—if you
agree, of course.'

'Thank you, Julia. I'll try to be worthy of her,' said
Melanie softly.

'Oh, you don't have to try, Melanie,' responded Julia.
'We've chosen her godparents very carefully,' she
added, 'for their very special qualities.' She gave
Melanie one of her old amused, enigmatic looks, but
Melanie could only wonder what qualities she could
possibly have to match those of the lovely Miranda.

'Do you feel able to receive visitors yet?'

Julia settled herself back against the pillows, tranquil
and radiant despite her lost night's sleep and the long
labour behind her. 'Send them up!' she smiled.

A murmur of subdued excitement issued from the
living room as Melanie pushed open the door. A cork

leapt out of a champagne bottle with a loud explosion.

'What timing!' Professor Young greeted her. 'First glass to Melanie, the best midwife in London!' he ordered gaily.

Daniel Davenport, his back turned to the rest of the room, was pouring the champagne into waiting glasses on the sideboard. He handed one to Melanie at last, avoiding her eyes, then one to Professor Young, then one to Miranda. The latter stood up gracefully from her seat near the French windows, took her glass and smiled radiantly at him. The consultant handed Toby Robertson a glass too.

'Well, I think if Julia's ready, we should take these upstairs,' said the Professor, looking at Melanie.

Melanie nodded and managed a smile. Her hand slipped up the cool stem of her champagne glass and she grasped it more tightly. I must keep a hold on myself, she thought.

Upstairs, she toasted the baby and Julia, then stood in an agony of embarrassment while the Professor proposed a 'long-overdue' toast to her. Daniel Davenport and Miranda exchanged a glace during his speech which Melanie could not read, but which increased her agony. Then Daniel smiled his beatific smile at Julia's sister's empty glass and the rueful glance she gave it.

'To the god-parents . . .' Professor Young was beginning.

'Oh, come on, Malcolm,' protested Miranda in her rich, husky voice, 'we're not at the Royal College annual do now. My glass needs refilling!'

The Professor was drowned in a general hubbub of glass clinking and champagne flowing. All that was left of his speech was his happy smile.

Melanie excused herself as soon as she decently could from this peculiarly painful family occasion, said her goodbyes and escaped into the cool evening outside. Toby caught her up on the drive.

'You must be shattered,' he said. 'I'll drive you home. You can pick up your car tomorrow.'

CHAPTER TEN

' . . . It's what I always say about these elderly prima gravidas—they take a wee bit longer, but they get there just the same. Of course, age is no contra-indication for home delivery, but you try telling your average obstetrician that! Living in the Dark Ages, most of them. While they pretend they're in the vanguard of social change and scientific progress . . .'

'Yes, Toby.'

'Of course, it happens to help if you're a midwife yourself. Mrs Young, for example, seemed to manage her own delivery, didn't she? I mean, I know you won't mind my saying this, Mella, but she was in charge, wasn't she? No doubt about it. And a fine job we made of it under her direction! She's quite a woman, eh, Melanie?'

'Yes, Toby.'

If this was the effect that a couple of glasses of champagne had on Toby Robertson, Melanie hoped for Rachel's sake that he didn't drink too much at the wedding.

'I thought we'd have to shift things on a bit at one stage, but then she bucked up a bit and, violà—a daughter! I hear she's named her after you, Mella. Well done. Quite right too . . .'

Melanie thought she had never been quite so pleased to see the tired summer foliage of Bedford Park. She gritted her teeth and heard out the remainder of Toby's impressions of Julia's delivery, interposing polite, apt replies when appropriate. She resisted the temptation to remind him that it had been she who had actually officiated at this event, and contented herself with the thought that the flat was four, three, two streets away. Once there, she thanked him effusively for the lift and almost leapt out of the car.

'Hey, hold on! I'm coming up too!' protested Toby.

Upstairs, Rachel greeted them, looking ravishing in a pale pink dress and smelling as cool and fragrant as a spring morning.

'Hi there! Fresh from the fray? God, you do look hot and sticky, Mella. You poor soul! I got off early. Nothing doing these days in SCBU. What are you two doing together?' She glowered playfully at Toby.

'We've just been delivering one of our joint patients,' announced Toby. 'Professor Young's wife actually,' he added.

Rachel looked astonished, then turned to Melanie for confirmation of the news. Melanie controlled her anger —just. For almost nine months she had been responsible for the care of Julia Young, and she had not betrayed her confidence to anyone.

'You haven't really been looking after the Prof.'s wife, have you, Mella?' Rachel prompted.

'I don't know if anyone at Lessing Lane officially knows yet,' Melanie replied. 'Perhaps it would be best if we let the Professor spread the good news himself.'

'I won't breathe a word. But how super! Boy or girl?'

'It's a little girl,' Melanie told her.

'You look exhausted, Mella,' said Rachel. 'It's just as well we're going out—you can have a nice peaceful time. It must have been a terrible strain on you keeping all this a secret for so long. Toby'll fill me in on all the gory details.'

'Yes,' agreed Melanie resignedly, 'I expect he will.' She mustered a smile. 'Have a nice time, both of you. Rachel, he's already been drinking, I warn you.'

Rachel looked fondly at Toby, who was beaming.

'Thank you, Mella,' she said, 'I'll bear that in mind.' She took Toby's arm and they went out.

Melanie watched from the bay window while they drove away. And then she watched while the fine late summer afternoon settled slowly into evening. The air remained still and warm, disturbed only by occasional birdsong and the low hum of aircraft high in the deep blue sky.

She did not know how long she stood there, her mind empty. Then she stirred herself. This is just anticlimax, she thought. I must do something. This inertia is terrible.

The telephone shocked her into life.

'Melanie? It's me. I've just met Toby and Rachel in The Foresters and she said you were sitting at home all alone after your triumph. Congratulations on the safe arrival . . .'

Melanie's mind clicked slowly to Joe Peters. He seemed far away, in another world.

'. . . so I thought I'd buy you a drink to celebrate. How about it?'

She cleared her throat.

'Melanie? Shall I pick you up?'

She hesitated.

'No, thank you, Joe. It's very nice of you, but I'm just too tired to enjoy anything. I'm sorry and all that . . .'

'Mella, you're not still worried about . . .'

'No, Joe,' Melanie said firmly. 'No,' she said more gently, 'it's not that. I'm just tired, that's all.'

'Okay, Melanie, I can take a hint. Cheers!'

The telephone went dead.

Melanie felt hot tears gathering behind her eyelids. She felt that if she let them fall they would be followed by more and she would never be able to stop crying.

She went into the bathroom and showered. Feeling slightly better, she sprayed her neck and arms with her favourite toilet water. In her bedroom, she slipped into the black dress that she had bought in Brighton. She had not worn it until now. The brief bodice and full skirt made it cool and comfortable. She slid her toes into some old leather thong sandals and put her purse, some sunglasses and her comb into the pockets. Then she slipped out of the flat, almost guiltily.

It was a long dusty walk to the river. She felt alone, free and unencumbered. She was a gypsy without a family or a home and, like a traveller, she revelled in her freedom. Nobody knew who she was or where she was. She did not know or care what strange urge had led her to dress and walk out into the street as if towards some secret rendezvous. She did not care. Her restlessness gave the familiar walk an enchanted character.

Nobody seemed to realise the trance that she was in. In this great moving metropolis, nobody thought anything odd. There were so many strange peoples here that even the extraordinary was commonplace. People imagined, as she walked along alone, that she was going to meet her fiancé or friend; that she would spend the evening as thousands would, sipping ice-cool drinks or regretting the length of a feature film in a hot and humid cinema.

Now and then, somebody caught her eye as they passed and acknowledged her presence on the planet with a thin smile or a friendly nod. But generally people were far too busy leading their own lives to give her more than a fleeting look.

How busy the world was! Melanie passed the huge new fire station opposite the bus station and crossed the busy High Road. Traffic was still pouring out of the city, although she felt the rush hour must be over by now. She glanced at her watch. It was half past six. She realised she was hungry.

All these husbands returning home to their wives, she thought as the file of neat cars with their white-shirted occupants flitted past her. All these happy suburban families. Suddenly the world seemed populated entirely with happy families—a world which even Rachel was soon to join and which seemed so mercilessly to exclude her.

And yet she knew it was not so. Passing the rows of dilapidated Victorian terrace houses, she knew that families as well as buildings fell. She knew that marriages failed and caused great pain and sorrow, despite the feelings that began them and the work that both partners put in. She was no rosy-cheeked schoolgirl when it came to romance.

And perhaps, she reflected, she never had been. Perhaps her childhood, the divorce of her parents and then their deaths had accustomed her early to the harsh realities of life. She had not suffered openly; she had been well cared for by kind relatives. But she had absorbed much before she reached her teens.

She did not feel sad about it. She felt as though some strange service had been done her. Now she knew that this was why she had refused to be deflected from her career and why she would not settle for the first man who came along.

She had watched her friends and fellow nurses and midwives through their many love affairs with interest, sometimes even with wonder. She had worried about herself, and had suffered goodnatured teasing. She had had enough of all that.

After all, if she was to spend the rest of her life single, she could do worse than to dedicate it to midwifery. No, whatever happened to her, she realised, she would always be a midwife. It was not an option to be thrown aside, it was central to her life. And what could be more satisfying? Her mind flew back to the events of today.

But she did not want to think about Julia now; the new baby, the godparents . . .

Kew Bridge was in sight; Melanie could see beyond it the greenery on the other side of the River Thames. Her pace quickened slightly, then slowed again as the warm air filled her lungs. It would be good to sit down on the grass. She would buy herself a cool drink on the Green.

On the crown of the bridge she stopped and leaned her elbows on the parapet, looking down into the murky waters of the Thames. They said it was so clean now that they had caught salmon the previous year, but that was hard to believe.

The many motorboats had left their mark on the banks: great raw eroded gashes where the banks had been worn away by their backwash. But ducks and a pair of swans drifted lightly downstream towards her, fishing lazily as they did so.

Swans mate for life, thought Melanie. She took her attention carefully away from this thought and focused it instead on a rowing eight which had appeared around the bend of the river towards Chiswick Bridge. Melanie marvelled at the discipline that drove their oars into the water with such perfect synchronisation. From the far bank, the coach yelled his instructions to the oarsmen through a loudhailer, and they were echoed by the little cox at the end of the boat.

They rushed beneath the bridge with a swish of blades. She traced the ripples which they made as they spread gently out towards the shores. Melanie had always found water so calming. It was so unchanging, and yet always in motion. She realised that the noise of the traffic behind her had diminished and that evening was establishing itself.

Slowly she wandered down towards Kew Green. She soon saw that she was not the only person who had been drawn to the trees and grass this evening. Beneath the trees along the edges of the Green, wherever there was a pub, the grass was covered in people. One or two ice-cream vans were dotted around the Green and were obviously doing a roaring trade.

Children ran between the trees, sucking ice lollies. Babies sat up uncertainly in their prams, covering their faces in ice-cream. Several games of football were in simultaneous progress, with athletic and enthusiastic small field players and rather less active, pint-carrying paternal goalkeepers.

Women in summer dresses sat in the grass or carried bottles of Coke and bags of crisps to younger members of the family. The scene was as timeless as the river: English summer as it has always been.

Melanie turned towards one of the pubs which stood slightly back from the Green and did not look so crowded. It was almost next door to the little shop where Julia had bought the silver teething ring. Julia. Julia and her house, her baby, her family . . .

Well, she would go and see Julia tomorrow, and she would continue to see her safely through her post-natal care until the final visit in six weeks' time. At last, Melanie faced the thought that she had been avoiding for these past two hours or more: the thought that that would be that. No more working or walking in these exalted circles. She must accept that the invitation to be a godmother was a kind gesture on Julia's part, and that was all. No more regular contact with professors' wives or consultant obstetricians—at least, not in the way to which she had become accustomed recently.

Or had she become accustomed to it? She wandered into the dark bar and bought herself a glass of grapefruit juice. Thinking about it, she realised that she had not really relaxed since the day that Julia Young had first appeared at the practice. But was this to do with Julia, or was it more to do with the uneasy relationship it had thrown her into with Daniel Davenport?

No, it was not Julia. She knew in her heart of hearts that her friendship with Julia Young was real and transcended all barriers. She knew that Julia had not named her baby after her, or asked her to be a godmother, as a mere gesture of gratitude.

She knew that it was all to do with Daniel Davenport, and that she had to face that. And what irony that she would have to stand next to him at the christening—for he was bound to be a godfather to the baby. More smiles, more toasts, more secret looks exchanged between him and Miranda . . .

Melanie found a seat at an empty table in the last of the sun. She put her sunglasses on to stop her eyes from pricking in the light. They were stinging with tiredness. She surveyed the couples lying side by side in the grass, talking, sipping their beer and making daisy chains for one another's hair.

She watched absentmindedly while a long white car nosed its way over the crown of Kew Bridge, then it was lost in the trees. She noted its reappearance a couple of seconds later, then its slow cruise around the far end of the Green. It was quite a startling car—so sleek and white amongst its more pedestrian fellows on the road. Amused, she saw it held up by a crowd of children at an ice-cream van, and then it slid forward again towards the corner where she sat.

And then she recognised the driver. Daniel got out of the Porsche and walked slowly towards where she sat, looking casually about him as he did so, his shirt sleeves rolled up, his jacket slung across his shoulder. As he drew near, he lifted his eyebrows and smiled a lopsided smile at her, gesturing towards one of the empty chairs at her table.

'May I?'

Melanie took off her glasses. 'Of course, do . . .' She did not know what she was saying.

'Well, it's been a long hard search and a safe arrival. Here you are, as large as life and twice as beautiful.' He looked hard and long at Melanie, then his eyes softened.

Melanie blushed and gulped her mouthful of grapefuit juice dregs.

'A long search? For me?' she queried.

'For you, midwife Melanie—a poem,' he replied laconically. 'May I get you a drink?'

'Thank you.'

'Well? What?'

Melanie searched her brain for an appropriate answer, but could find none. Just confusion and questions and more confusion. He was searching her face patiently for clues.

'Fruit juice,' she said suddenly.

He looked at her again with amusement, then strolled off in the direction of the bar, his hands in his pockets.

What's he doing? Melanie asked herself the same question ten times. What's he doing here? He reappeared with their drinks.

'Fruit juice,' he said, putting it down in front of her. 'You'll have to excuse my drinking a pint of beer. All that insipid champagne gives me a raging thirst.'

She stared at him while he drained half a pint in one go.

'As I said,' he continued, 'I've been looking everywhere for you. Went to the flat—nobody there. And I've been scouring the streets ever since.'

'You must have passed me,' murmured Melanie. 'I walked here very slowly, via the High Road.'

'No. I did a round trip, all the back roads. I thought you might be wandering around locally, visiting friends.'

Melanie smiled at the thought as she compared his image of her with the reality of the past hour. She found herself sliding between uncontrolled pleasure at his sudden appearance and a vague sense of discomfort at the possible reason for it.

'But what did you want to find me for?' she asked.

Daniel Davenport looked appraisingly at her, as though he were about to ask her a testing professional question in an oral examination. A crowd of young people suddenly took over the table next to theirs, jostling, joking and shouting orders over their heads.

'Good God,' exploded Dr Davenport, 'this place is about as private and secluded as the staff canteen at Lessing Lane! Can't we go somewhere else?'

Melanie made no move, except to sip her juice. Her heart was missing beats quite regularly, but if he was here to tick her off, she would rather have people about and not be alone with him.

'I wanted to ask you something,' said the consultant, exasperation in his tone.

He took another draught of his beer. Melanie felt a flicker of panic pass through her, then she comforted herself with the fleeting thought that, whatever he had to say about her, or to her, nothing could adversely affect the outcome of Julia's confinement now. Then, as if she was dreaming it, she saw the little silver head of a bear beneath a mother-of-pearl ring. It was poking precariously out of Daniel's shirt pocket. The sight was so incongruous that she almost laughed. The doctor followed her eyes and put his hand up instinctively to his pocket, but he was too late to stop the toy from plopping noisily and unceremoniously into his pint.

A giggle gathered around the table next to them, at least two of the occupants of which had seen this incident, and the consultant reddened with annoyance and confusion. Melanie watched, transfixed, this unheard-of event, then modestly composed her face.

'Can you still drink your beer?' she asked.

He did not answer her. Instead, he fished out the teething ring and handed it roughly to her. 'This is yours anyway.'

'Mine?' she queried.

'Now can we go somewhere quieter?'

'Why have you given me this?' asked Melanie.

'Because Julia said it was better than no ring at all.'

Melanie frowned and joined him standing up beside the table. She could not understand what he was talking about.

'And she also said, if you want to know, that it was about time I got my bloody act together.'

Melanie glanced at his face and burst into genuine giggles.

'Julia doesn't mince her words!' she laughed.

'She certainly doesn't when she's just given birth to a daughter.'

Melanie allowed him to put his arm around her shoulders and lead her away from the pub. She still hardly knew what was happening, but the ridiculous episode at the pub had relaxed her and made her almost uncaring of what he was going to say to her. She had entered a state of stupid happiness that asked no more questions of her. She was too tired and too drained of emotion to do anything but enjoy the moment.

Daniel led her away from the main road, and five minutes later they entered the garden of a restaurant so secluded that the entrance was hidden from the street. It was really a perfect place; deserted, with one or two tables beneath fairy lights slung from the trees, and inside an intimate dining area visible from where they stood. Melanie was led to the seats beneath the trees where she sat down. He sat down opposite her.

'I don't really understand,' she murmured. 'We seem always to have had difficulty understanding one another, but now you're really confusing me. If you're angry with me over something, or want to question me over my performance professionally today, then please tell me straight out . . . Why have you brought me here? Please explain all this, Daniel . . .'

Now she had used his first name. What was happening to her? She still clasped the tiny silver bear in one hand, but neither it nor the environment nor the company seemed real.

The consultant drew his chair closer and took both of her hands in his.

'It's very simple, Melanie. I want to marry you.'

She shook her head disbelievingly, but he only smiled.

'Yes, I know,' he said, 'I have a good deal of explaining to do. Please hear me out, Melanie. First, you should know that I've been married before. It was a bad marriage, after a misspent youth, and the only excuse I have for that is that I didn't meet you then . . .'

'But Miranda!' interrupted Melanie in spite of herself. 'I thought you . . .'

'Melanie, please don't interrupt me. Miranda is Julia's sister . . .'

'I know that. But . . .'

'She's married to an old friend of mine, an officer in the Merchant Navy,' he continued quietly. 'He does long hauls to and fro from the Middle East with oil. I often escort Miranda while he's away. She's a lively girl—like her sister. She works hard as a Senior Registrar at Bart's and she likes to play sometimes too. Her husband knows that, and the arrangement is very happy for everyone. We all met many years ago.

'Melanie, I have to tell you this. I want you to know everything. You have to know.'

Melanie had never seen him so serious. She gazed at him.

'Melanie, my wife was very unstable, and she longed for a child. We had trouble, and went through all the usual tests and infertility investigations. When the doctors down in the West Country couldn't advise us any more, she was referred to Professor Young up here in London for a specialist opinion. He was a consultant then, but already famed for his work on the psychology of pregnancy and infertility. At last, to cut a long story short, my wife conceived.'

Daniel paused and took a deep breath.

'And your child?' Melanie whispered.

Daniel hesitated, then said in a low voice: 'He died soon after birth. Nobody could explain it. He seemed perfectly healthy at birth. It was a cot death. Nobody could have prevented it.'

'How terrible! I'm so sorry,' Melanie responded.

'It was terrible,' Daniel spoke slowly, as if remembering, 'and my wife never got over it. I found that I could come to terms with it, but she couldn't. She divorced me, still blaming me somehow. And to my shame, I blamed her.'

Melanie stared at him. 'How could you?' she queried.

'He was born at home,' Daniel returned. 'I worried and wondered if things might have been different if . . . I was a general surgeon at the time and with the usual suspicions of medics in other areas . . . I wondered if the obs and gynae men knew what they were doing. You know how we all are.' He waited for her reaction. She nodded mutely.

'But Julia and Malcolm finally convinced me that nothing could have been done to save the baby. I retained my fears about home confinement—but I don't have to tell you about that. The Youngs have been wonderful friends to me ever since, Melanie—I can't tell you how wonderful. And since I saw you, Melanie . . .'

He lifted her hand, the one that still clasped the bear, and kissed it softly. Then he opened it and took the toy, then kissed the palm.

'It's a long time since I confided my feelings about you

to the Youngs, Melanie. And yet I didn't know how to approach you. I knew you thought me completely un-reasonable, and I knew that I had an irrational fear of what you chose to do professionally, even though it was a doctor who delivered my own child. But you seemed so self-sufficient always, so sure of your own ground, so unapproachable . . .'

She shook her head again, again amazed at how she must appear to him. But he laid his fingers gently across her lips, forbidding her to speak yet.

'Melanie, it's so stupid, but I got into such a state of cowardice, in case you would reject me. I promised the Youngs that by today, by the time the child was born, I should have . . . I would have . . .'

He slipped off his chair so that he could take her face in his hands. His lips moved lightly over her hair, her forehead, her eyes . . .

'Will you marry me, Melanie?'

Melanie met the passion in his clouded blue-grey eyes, the conflicting youth and experience in his expressive face, and loved it all, as she had always done.

'Yes,' she responded simply, 'I will.'

They stood and kissed; a kiss so complete and shared that neither knew how to end it. Melanie felt Daniel's arms tighten around her and the world retreated.

'You're trembling,' he murmured at last.

A soft, discreet cough nearby made them both turn around. The waiter met their stare with apology in his quiet smile. 'Er—shall I lay your table out here, Dr Davenport, sir, or will you eat inside?'

Daniel glanced at Melanie's bare shoulders and gave her a protective hug. 'Indoors, I think, Melanie?'

'Yes, indoors,' said Melanie.

The waiter disappeared. The breeze that had been playing through the trees had turned chilly. Daniel drew Melanie to him once more. 'There'll be many summer nights,' he whispered. He took her gently by the waist and she knew with wonder the closeness of his embrace. All her senses responded to this man as she had always known they would. But she knew now what she had always waited for—this whole feeling, this complete mutual melting. She whispered his name and felt his instant response to her.

They parted by mutual understanding and moved, arm in arm, towards the restaurant. Daniel dropped the little silver bear into her hand again, and she put it into her pocket.

'We godparents need to liaise very, very closely, you know.' He hugged her close to him as he opened the door to the restaurant. 'Continuity of spiritual care,' he explained with a grin.

Melanie smiled at him.

'And good practice,' he added wickedly.

SAY IT WITH ROMANCE